Copyright © 2025 Amy Rose

This novel is entirely a work of fiction. The names, characters, and incidents portrayed in it are the work of the author's imagination. Any resemblance to actual persons, living or dead, events or localities is entirely coincidental.

All rights reserved. No part of this publication may be reproduced, stored, or transmitted in any form or by any means, electronic, mechanical, photocopying, recording, scanning, or otherwise, without written permission from the publisher. It is illegal to copy this book, post it to a website, or distribute it by any other means without permission.

The scanning, uploading and distribution of this book without permission is a theft of the authors intellectual property. If you would like permission to use material form from the book (other than for review purposes) please contact Amy at hello@ amyjudithrose.com

ISBN: 979-8-9893447-5-8

THE DADDY SECRET
Series

BROKEN
Vows

BOOK ONE

AMY ROSE

THE DADDY SECRET
Series

BROKEN
Vows

BOOK ONE

AMY ROSE

Content Warnings

This story contains cheating from a spouse, and pregnancy.

This story also contains cancer / death information about a parent.

Chapter One

STEAM LEAKS OUT FROM UNDER THE BATHROOM DOOR, bringing the smell of his vanilla soap with it. I open the door and put his clothes on the toilet seat, making sure they're laid out nicely for when he's done.

"Here are your clothes, honey,"

"Thank you, Alexis,"

Our wedding photo on the wall catches my eye, me in my white dress, Jeremy in his tux, both of us grinning like we had the whole world figured out. Below it sits the wooden box he gave me on our first Christmas together, filled with art supplies and an engraved note that reads "For my future famous artist." I'd been waitressing then, sketching on napkins between serving tables. He believed in my art before I did.

The box sits dusty now, untouched for months. Just like my sketchbooks, my dreams of a career in art seem to have faded into something I'll get around to "someday." he doesn't ask about my art anymore.

I'm closing his lunch box when he walks into the kitchen wearing his bright high vis orange work shirt, dark blue jeans, and dark brown steel toe boots. His dark hair is dripping water onto his shoulders, and his eyes still look heavy with sleep.

He opens the lunch box and looks inside before his eyes narrow a bit. "Where are my granola bars?" his tone coming out annoyed.

"I'm sorry. I didn't know we were out. I'll get some today."

He sighs and gives me a quick kiss. "Thanks, Lex. See you tonight."

"Have a good day," I call after him. I lock the door behind him before going back to the kitchen, pouring myself a small hot coffee.

The familiar squeak of the third board from the refrigerator takes me back to our first night in this house. Jeremy had carried me over the threshold, both of us laughing as he nearly tripped on the uneven floor.

"We'll fix that," he'd promised, setting me down gently. We never did. Somehow the creaky boards became part of our story, like the chip in the kitchen counter from moving day and the slightly crooked cabinet door that never quite closes right. I run my fingers along that chip now. Five years of marriage marked in the small imperfections of our home.

Sometimes I wonder if he even notices how hard I

try by making sure he has his lunch prepared every morning, that he has his wallet and phone on him before he leaves, keeping the house tidy, or if it's just become normal for him.

We used to stay up late planning vacations, watching movies, making recipes in the cook book his mother gave us. Over time, the power company took more and more of him. Longer hours, more responsibilities, endless overtime. The plans we made gather dust like my unused paint brushes.

I know I won't fall back asleep and if I do, I'll waste the whole day doing nothing. I walk around the house, picking things up as I go, dirty dishes, garbage, little things like that. I make the bed, fluff the pillows, and sit down to watch TV before I have to leave later.

The day passes in a blur of errands and chores. I get the granola bars and some snacks for myself. I hate going to the grocery store - everything costs so much now. But we need to eat.

I take extra time organizing the pantry, then settle on the couch and FaceTime Lilly, needing to hear a friendly voice.

She answers after a few rings, her smiling face popping up on my screen. "Hey, Lex!" she says cheerly. "How's it going?"

We've been best friends forever. We've been friends since grade school, and our friendship has lasted through high school, college, and marriage.

I sigh and run my hand through my hair. "Hey.

It's been one of those days. I forgot his snacks, and he got annoyed, so I ran out and bought them before he comes home."

Her face softens with a small smile. "That sounds rough. How's he doing?"

"He's fine, just the usual. It's me that feels off. I think he's so wrapped up in work that he doesn't notice how little time we spend together."

"Have you two tried talking about it?"

"Not really," I admit. "I keep hoping things will get better on their own. Maybe once we're past this busy time, things will go back to how they used to be."

She shakes her head, her brunette curls bouncing with the motion. "Lex, you can't just wait for things to magically fix themselves. You need to communicate. Maybe set aside some time for just the two of you, even if it's just for dinner or a weekend getaway."

I have tried to plan things like this before, but he either doesn't feel well or wants to go hang out with his family.

"Yeah, you're right."

She's always been the person I can trust aside from Jeremy or family. I don't really have a lot of friends. Pretty much everyone I knew and graduated with five years ago went their separate ways.

I didn't really have much of a plan after graduation. I knew I enjoyed creating art, writing, crafting, graphic design, but five years later I've never really gone anywhere with them as a business.

Sometimes, not having much of a plan makes me feel like a failure. I don't want to rely on my husband for income, but it seems to have fallen that way.

I look at the time on my phone and realize it's already reaching 6 o'clock in the afternoon. "Hey, I've got to prepare dinner, talk later?"

"Yeah! Talk later!"

We hang up, and I place my phone down on the couch and walk into the kitchen. He's been requesting tacos for a while now, but I haven't been wanting to make them as it's a lot of work. But tonight I want to impress him, and cooking what he wants may ease the tension a bit. Maybe making tacos tonight will mean we won't argue when he gets home.

I understand he's tired after working a physically demanding job, but he doesn't say no to his siblings or friends when they want to hang out. Only for me does he hesitate to make plans.

I miss him. I miss us.

I hear the front door knob click, and Jeremy walks in the house. I've already set our plates with a couple tacos.

"Hi baby, how was your day?"

"Good, have a slight headache though," he says as he sits down to take off his shoes.

"I'm sorry. Have you had any medicine?"

"Yeah." He slips off his shoes and puts them on the shoe rack.

"I made tacos and also got the granola bars today."

"Sounds good baby. Hey, could you grab me some clothes? I'm going to take a bath."

He's been taking baths more often lately.

"Yeah, I'll be right back." I head toward our bedroom and grab him some fresh boxers, a shirt and some shorts, and place them on the toilet seat.

"Could you also run the bath?" he asks from the living room.

"Yeah!" I turn the knob and watch the water fill the tub as I add some muscle relaxing Epsom salt in as well, knowing it helps him relax even more after a long day at work. I head back to the living room, sit on the couch, and begin eating my tacos alone as he heads to the bathroom with his plate.

I guess making dinner didn't help make a happier evening.

An hour later, the bathroom door opens, and he emerges wrapped in a towel, his skin flushed from the hot bath. I look up from my half-eaten taco on the couch.

"Feel better?" I ask, trying to keep my voice light.

He nods, running a hand through his damp hair. "Yeah, thanks. The bath helped."

I watch as he moves to the kitchen, opening the fridge and peering inside. "Did you pick up any soda while you were out today?"

I feel a pang of guilt. "No, I'm sorry. I forgot."

He sighs, closing the fridge door a bit harder than necessary. "It's fine. I'll pick some up tomorrow."

The silence feels heavy. I want to say something to bridge the gap between us, but the words don't come.

He places two more tacos on his plate. "I'm going to eat in bed and watch some TV."

As the bedroom door closes behind him, I'm left alone in the living room.

The house is too quiet, despite Jeremy's presence in the next room. I can hear the muffled sound of the TV through the wall.

My phone buzzes with a text from Lilly:

LILLY

Hey, how is everything?

I stare at the message, unsure how to respond.

ME

Jeremy's tired. Watching TV in bed.

LILLY

Want to meet for coffee tomorrow?
My treat.

It's tempting, but I hesitate.

ME

Thanks, but I've got a lot to do around the house.

I reply, already regretting it.

LILLY

Okay, but don't forget to take care of yourself too.

I should go to bed, curl up next to Jeremy, and pretend everything's normal.

Instead, I find myself in my art room. My art supplies are in the closet, untouched for months. I pull out a sketchpad and pencils, their familiar weight both comforting and intimidating.

I settle at the desk and open to a blank page, taking a deep breath and begin to draw.

As I begin drawing, something inside me unwinds. The lines start shaky but grow more confident. I lose track of time, lost in creating. It's past midnight when I look up. The sketch isn't great - just the view from our kitchen window - but it's something. A start.

I tiptoe to the bedroom, careful not to wake Jeremy. He's sprawled across his side, one arm in the space where I should be. I slide under the covers, fitting against his warmth.

Chapter Two

The alarm blares at 3:45 a.m jolting me awake. I fumble for my phone, silencing it before it can wake Jeremy. He stirs slightly but doesn't wake, his breathing steady and deep.

I slip out of bed, the cool air sending goosebumps up my legs. The house is dark and quiet as I make my way to the kitchen, guided by muscle memory more than sight.

As I prepare his lunch, my mind wanders to last night's sketch. It wasn't much, but it felt good to create something again.

I place his neatly packed lunch box on the counter and start the coffeemaker. The rich aroma fills the kitchen, a small comfort in the early morning darkness.

His footsteps in the hallway signal his approach. He enters the kitchen, eyes still heavy with sleep, and reaches for the coffeepot.

"Morning," he mumbles, pouring himself a cup.

"Good morning, sleep well?"

He shrugs, taking a long sip of coffee. "Alright, I guess. You came to bed late."

"Yeah, I was…" I hesitate, unsure whether to mention the drawing. "Just lost track of time."

"I'm going to shower."

I hear the bathroom door close and the shower start and move to lay out his clothes. As I place them on the bed, my gaze falls on the framed photo on his nightstand. It's us on our honeymoon. I pick it up, studying our younger faces. We looked so happy, so full of hope for the future. When did that change? I shake my head, grabbing the clothes and bringing them into the bathroom, placing them onto the toilet seat.

"Your lunch is on the counter. I packed extra granola bars."

"Thanks," he says, pulling on his shirt. "I might be late tonight. We've got a big project coming up."

"Oh, okay. Should I keep dinner warm for you?"

He shakes his head. "Don't bother. I'll grab something on the way home."

He finishes dressing and grabs his lunch box from the counter. He gives me a quick peck on the cheek before heading out the door. "See you later," he calls over his shoulder.

"Have a good day," I call out, but the door swings shut with a thud, cutting me off. The house feels emptier than usual as I move through my morning routine. I straighten up the house, wrestling with a mountain of laundry, somehow finding the will to care for these everyday chores.

By mid-morning, I find myself back in the office, staring at last night's sketch. I grab my phone and snap a picture, sending it to Lilly with the message:

ME

Drew this last night.

With a blank canvas before me, I gaze intently, holding my pencil above the page, like it's holding its breath, waiting for the lines to take shape and bring the image to life under my hand. I've been sitting here for an hour, and still… nothing.

With a sigh, I lower my pencil and glance at the clock on my phone, 9:37 AM. Jeremy would have been at work for over two hours by now. Even after five months, I still catch myself thinking about his schedule, as if it matters anymore.

I shake my head, trying to dislodge the memory of our life together. Focus, Alexis. This is your chance to create something new, something entirely yours.

But the white expanse of the canvas seems to mock me. I set down my pencil and canvas, making my way toward the kitchen.

I pour myself a cup of coffee, inhaling the rich brew. It's one of the few pleasures I allow myself these days.

My phone buzzes, cutting through my thoughts. I

glance at the screen and feel a small smile tug at my lips. Lilly.

"Hey, you," I answer, grateful for the distraction.

"Please tell me you're not still in your pajamas." Her bubbly voice comes through the speaker.

I glance down at my paint-splattered sweatpants and oversized t-shirt. "I'm not still in my pajamas," I lie, unable to keep the amusement out of my voice.

"Liar," she laughs. "Come on, it's a beautiful day outside. You can't spend another one cooped up in that house."

I bite my lip, glancing towards the window. The sunlight does look inviting. "I don't know, Lil. I was trying to paint…"

"And how's that going?" she asks knowingly.

I sigh. "Not great."

"Then it's settled. I'm picking you up. We're going to Rosie's in thirty minutes. No excuses."

Before I can protest, she hangs up. I stare at my phone for a moment. She has been my lifeline these past few months, dragging me out of my shell when all I want to do is hide away.

I drink the last of my coffee and head to my bedroom to change. I catch sight of myself in the full-length mirror. The woman staring back at me looks tired, a little lost. Am I beautiful to him? Am I enough for him? Why am I not happy? What is wrong with me? I shake the thoughts and finish getting ready before taking a deep breath, squaring my shoulders.

"You've got this, Alexis," I tell myself. "One day at a time."

Chapter Three

The familiar scent of coffee and freshly baked pastries envelops me as I walk into Rosie's Cafe.

We take a seat in a corner booth.

She leans forward, her elbows on the table. "How are you doing?"

I sigh, fiddling with the menu in front of me. "I'm... okay, I guess," I mumble. "It's just been like..."

"Rough? Yeah, I get it. But hey, you're here, you're dressed—"

"Barely," I interject, gesturing to my hastily thrown-on jeans and oversized t-shirt.

"—and you're out of the house," she continues, undeterred. "I'd call that a win."

Before I can respond, a waiter appears at our table, his pen poised over his notepad. "What can I get for you ladies today?"

"I'll have a caramel latte and a blueberry muffin,"

"Um, just a black coffee for me, thanks," I mutter, not meeting the waiter's eyes.

As he walks away, Lilly kicks me gently under the table. "Seriously? Just coffee? You need to eat something."

I shrug, feeling defensive. "I'm not hungry."

"When was the last time you had a proper meal?"

I wrack my brain, trying to remember. "I... I had a taco recently?"

Her eyes widen. "That's it. I'm ordering you a sandwich. And don't even think about arguing."

As if on cue, the waiter returns with our drinks. Before I can protest, she adds a turkey sandwich to our order. The waiter nods and disappears again, leaving me to stare accusingly at my best friend.

"You didn't have to do that," I grumble, wrapping my hands around the warm mug of coffee.

"Yes, I did," she says firmly. "Now, tell me about this drawing you sent me. It was good." I feel a flutter of pride at her words, quickly followed by a wave of uncertainty. "It was just a quick sketch. Nothing special."

"Bullshit," she declares, loud enough to earn us a few curious glances from nearby tables. "You've got talent. You always have. Why aren't you doing more with it?"

I take a sip of my coffee, buying time before I have to answer. I don't know why I stopped drawing. It just seemed to fade away, like so many other things in my life lately.

"I don't know," I admit finally. "It's been so long. I'm not even sure I remember how to really draw anymore."

Her face softens. "Oh, honey. That's not how it works. It's like riding a bike. You just need to get back on and start pedaling." As she speaks, the waiter returns with her muffin and my sandwich. The sight and smell of the food make my stomach growl embarrassingly loud, reminding me just how long it's been since I've eaten a proper meal.

"See? Your body knows what it needs. Now eat."

I take a bite of the sandwich, and it's like my taste buds have suddenly woken up. Before I know it, I've devoured half of it.

"So," she says, delicately wiping muffin crumbs from her lips, "what's stopping you from drawing more? And don't say Jeremy."

I nearly choke on my sandwich. "I wasn't going to say Jeremy," I lie, even though that's exactly where my mind went.

She furrows her brows. "Sure. Look, Lex, I know things have been tough with him lately, but you can't let that stop you from doing what you love."

"It's not just him, it's... everything. I feel stuck. Like I'm just going through the motions every day, waiting for something to change."

"And what if you're the change?" she asks, leaning forward. "What if picking up that pencil again is the first step to getting unstuck?"

I open my mouth to argue, but no words come out.

"Maybe it's time I start really drawing again."

Her smile widens. "That's my girl. Now, finish your sandwich. We've got an art supply store to visit."

THE BELL ABOVE THE ART STORE'S DOOR CHIMES AS LILLY drags me inside, her enthusiasm radiating off her in waves. The scent of fresh paper and paint hits me.

"Okay, where do we start?"

I can't help but chuckle at her excitement. "You realize I'm the artist here, right?"

She sticks her tongue out at me. "Details, details. Come on, let's go wild!"

As we wander down an aisle filled with sketchbooks, I run my fingers along the spines, feeling the different textures. "You know," I say, "I used to dream about having an unlimited budget in a place like this."

She grabs a leather-bound sketchbook off the shelf, holding it out to me like it's made of gold. "Well, consider this your fairy godmother moment. Any sketchbook you want, it's yours."

I raise an eyebrow. "No, that one's like fifty bucks."

"And?" she challenges. "Consider it an investment in your future as a famous artist."

I roll my eyes but can't keep the smile off my face. "Fine, but I'm buying my own pencils."

We make our way to the pencil section, where Lilly picks up a set of colorful markers. "Ooh, what about these?"

"For sketching?" I laugh. "Not unless I want my drawings to look like a kindergartener's art project."

She pouts playfully. "Hey, don't knock down kindergarten art."

As I'm examining a set of graphite pencils, she gasps dramatically. I look up to see her holding a ridiculously large paintbrush. "Lex! This is it! This is what your art has been missing!"

I can't hold back my laughter. "Oh yeah, because what every sketch artist needs is a paintbrush the size of their head."

She waves it around like a wand. "Alexis the Great, Master of Gigantic Brushstrokes!"

An elderly woman browsing nearby gives us a disapproving look, which only makes us laugh harder.

After what feels like hours of Lilly's antics and my half-hearted attempts to actually shop, we finally make it to the checkout with a respectable haul of supplies.

As we walk back to her car, arms filled with bags, she bumps her hip against mine. "See? Wasn't this more fun than moping at home?"

I nod, feeling lighter than I have in weeks. "Yeah, yeah, you were right. Don't let it go to your head."

As she pulls up in front of my house, I feel a twinge of reluctance to leave this bubble of happiness we've created.

She must sense my hesitation because she turns to me with a soft smile. "Hey, you've got this, okay? Just promise me you'll actually use those supplies."

I nod, gathering my bags. "I promise. Thanks for today. I mean it."

As I'm about to close the car door, she calls out, "See you later!"

I wave her bye and watch her drive away, then turn to head inside.

Chapter Four

I LOSE MYSELF IN THE LINES OF MY LATEST SKETCH, barely noticing the sunlight shifting across my desk throughout the afternoon. My hand moves almost of its own accord, filling page after page with designs that flow from my imagination. It's only when my stomach growls that I realize how much time has passed.

Glancing at the clock, I wince. It's almost 10 PM, and I promised to make dinner tonight. But where is Jeremy? I grab my phone and send him a text.

ME

Honey, is everything okay?

My back aches from hours of sketching. I should probably get up. What's the point of making a meal when we'll probably eat in silence, if we even eat together at all? Still, I promised. I pull out some meat and begin cooking.

Maybe tonight will be different. Maybe we can watch a movie or just talk over a glass of wine.

Anything to bridge this gap between us. I'm so lost in thought that I nearly slice my finger, the knife coming dangerously close to my skin.

The sound of the front door opening sends a jolt through me. I quickly wipe my hands on a dish towel and head to the living room.

"Hey," I say as he walks in, his pant buckle already loosened. "How was your day?"

He grunts in response, hanging up his hard hat by the door. "Long. Exhausting. The usual."

I bite my lip, watching as he collapses onto the couch, eyes already fixed on his phone.

"It's almost 10. Where were you?"

"Took longer than usual with some power lines."

"Want to watch a movie tonight?" I ask. "Or just talk for a bit? Since it's a Friday, we could stay up late?"

He looks up, his brow furrowing. "Alexis, I'm beat. Can't we just have a quiet night?"

Something in me snaps. "That's all we ever have!" I yell. "I just want to spend time with you! Even if it's just a movie in our bed!"

He sighs angrily, his face hardening. "I don't even have time for myself! I don't have time for anything anymore!" He kicks the empty soda box we left on the floor, sending it skidding across the room.

I feel the burn of tears welling in my eyes. This

isn't how I wanted this to go. It never is, but somehow, we always end up here. "We've barely spent any time together," I murmur, sinking onto the sofa.

He doesn't respond. He just sits there, staring at the wall, jaw clenched. The silence stretches between us, thick and suffocating.

"It's almost eleven." I say, standing up. "I'm going to head to bed after finishing cooking."

As I walk toward our bedroom to grab a hand towel from the clean laundry basket, I hear him padding behind me. I pause at the doorway, turning to face him. His eyes meet mine, and for a moment, I see a flicker of something—regret? Sadness? Before I can decipher it, he steps forward and wraps his arms around me.

I stiffen at first, surprised by the sudden contact, but then I melt into his embrace. We stand there for a long moment, neither of us speaking. There's still so much unsaid between us, so many issues to work through. But for now, this quiet moment of connection feels like a lifeline.

He pulls back slightly, his hand cupping my cheek. "I'm sorry," he places his hand on my shoulder. "I know I've been distant. It's just... work has been"

I place my finger on his lips, silencing him. "I know," I say softly. "We can talk about it tomorrow. For now, can we just... be together?"

He nods, the corner of his lips turning up.

I let go and give him a kiss, and head back into the kitchen to finish up dinner.

Chapter Five

Jeremy's at work, and I have nothing much to do aside from binge-watching some dramatic romance movie or taking a walk around the block. I might even go to the park.

But that's just me procrastinating more than anything. I should sit down in front of a blank canvas, painting or drawing, but I'm stuck. I have no inspiration or motivation unless it's one of those spur-of-the-moment things. I might feel okay for the first few minutes, maybe an hour, and then I lose the spark. I guess my life at home is boring.

I twist a strand of my hair around my finger, glancing at the half-finished sketch on the table. It's been staring at me for days now. I know what I want to create, but the energy isn't there. The idea of picking up the brush or a pencil feels heavy, so instead, I shift in my chair, letting it squeak as I swivel back to face my computer.

My phone buzzes, interrupting the silence, and I see Lilly's name pop up on my screen.

LILLY

Coffee tomorrow?

ME

Sure. Noon?

It's easier to agree to plans right now than to sit alone in this quiet house with my thoughts. Lately, it feels like Lilly's the only person who understands that something's been off with Jeremy and me.

I push my chair back and wander into the kitchen, pulling open the fridge. The cool air hits my face as I stare inside at the leftovers of last night's spaghetti and some salad from earlier in the week. Jeremy's been working late a lot. I used to make a point of cooking something special for him to come home to, but lately, I can't even bother to reheat what's already there.

I grab a cold bottle of water, its condensation clinging to my hand, and lean against the cool, smooth countertop, staring out the window. It's peaceful out there. I wish it felt like that inside me.

My phone buzzes again, and I glance down. Another text from Lilly.

LILLY

Yes! How's everything with Jeremy?

I bite my lip, feeling the familiar knot in my

stomach. What should I say? Things between Jeremy and me feel like they're unraveling slowly, like a sweater that's been pulled one thread at a time?

ME

Same old. Work has been keeping him busy.

The door clicks open, and I turn to see Jeremy walk in earlier than expected. His shirt slung over his arm, hair still damp with sweat from work. He pauses at the door, his eyes flicking over to me for a moment before dropping his keys on the table.

"You're back early," I say, leaning casually against the counter. My fingers grip the cool surface behind me.

"Yeah, finished up sooner than I thought," he replies, heading straight for the fridge without another glance. The door swings open, and I can hear the clink of bottles as he grabs a beer. He pops the cap off and takes a long sip before setting the bottle on the counter.

"Hungry?" I ask, already feeling the answer before the words leave my mouth.

"Nah, I'm good." His response is quick, dismissive, and I feel the space between us grow a little wider.

I open my mouth to say something more, but he cuts me off. "I'm gonna head out later. The guys wanna grab a drink." He says it like it's already decided.

"Oh." It comes out softer than I meant, and I straighten up, trying to mask the slight disappointment. "You just got home, though."

He shrugs, wiping his forehead with the back of his hand. "Yeah, but we've had this planned for a while."

I look at him for a moment, weighing my words. I want to ask him to stay, to suggest we spend some time together, but something in the way he's standing tells me it wouldn't make a difference. He's already out the door in his mind.

"Okay," I say finally, forcing a small smile. "I'll save you some dinner for later."

Jeremy nods, and without another word, heads to the bedroom to change. I listen to the sound of his footsteps fade down the hall, the dull thud of the bedroom door closing behind him. The kitchen feels emptier now, like the silence is creeping back in to fill the space he left behind.

I walk over to the stove and stir the pasta I'd started earlier, trying to distract myself. The smell of garlic and tomatoes fills the kitchen, but I barely register it. My mind's too full, running over every minor detail of our conversation—how he barely looked at me, how quick he was to leave.

Our relationship wasn't always like this. Dull, distant.

I SIT DOWN WITH MY PLATE OF PASTA, STARING AT THE TV. It's one of those romance movies where everything works out in the end, but I'm not really watching it. I'm just filling the space.

It's nearly 9 p.m., and there's no sign of Jeremy yet. I get up, rinse my dish, and leave the rest of the pasta on the stove. He'll eat it when he gets home, or he won't.

I wander into the bedroom, and for a moment, I stand there, staring at the bed we share. I'm not tired yet, but the thought of lying in it alone again makes me feel heavy.

I grab my sketchbook from the bedside table and head back to the living room, flipping through the pages. Each unfinished drawing stares back at me— pieces of something I can't quite complete. I pick up a pencil and hover over the blank space of a new page, but the inspiration won't come. Not tonight.

At least I tried.

Chapter Six

I scrunch my nose while walking into the cafe doors. The coffee here is always strong when they first open. Walking up to the counter, I order myself a mocha frappuccino. I go to sit down after purchasing and wait for Lilly to get here. I don't know exactly when she will be here this morning, but that's okay. I can sit here and wait. Better than sulking around at home.

I've been going to this local coffee shop ever since I was a little girl. My mom would bring me every morning before taking me to school and or heading to work. It was our bonding time.

I miss those moments. Cancer is a bitch. For seven years, my mother has been gone from this world and when she was first diagnosed with ovarian cancer, I was there by her side daily. Jeremy was there with me. He's always been my rock.

The door chimes and I look up to see Lilly waving

excitedly at me. She orders her coffee, then walks over, sitting across from me.

"Morning cheery!" I say.

"Hey girl! Did you draw anything new?" she gives me a stern look.

Shaking my head, I let out a sigh. "Nope. Blank canvas is mocking me, though."

Lilly leans forward, resting her elbows on the table, her eyes soft but insistent. "Seriously, Lex, talk to him. It's not just work, and you know it. You can't just sit here and let your thoughts run wild without knowing for sure."

I take a sip of my Frappuccino, feeling the chill of the ice hit my teeth. "I know, but... what if I'm wrong? What if I'm just making things up in my head because I'm stressed?"

She tilts her head and gives me that knowing look —the one that always makes me feel like she can see right through me. "Are you though? You've been married to him for five years. You know when something's off. And if you're wrong, great! But at least you'll know."

I stare out the window, watching as people pass by with their coffee cups and briefcases, rushing to start their days. Everything outside feels so normal, like life keeps moving at full speed while I'm stuck in some slow-motion haze. "It just feels like... if I confront him and I'm right, everything will fall apart. Again."

I shake my head slowly. No, I don't want to live

like this. Over time, the gap between Jeremy and me has started to grow. I'm so used to him being my rock, the one who was there through everything with my mom, but now… it's like I don't even know who he is anymore. Or maybe I'm just scared of who he's become.

She takes a sip of her coffee, eyeing me over the rim of her cup. "When was the last time you really talked to him? Not just the 'how was your day' stuff, but really talked?"

I pause, a knot of tension in my stomach struggling to remember. I can't pinpoint the last time we had an actual conversation, one where we weren't just talking about work or errands or what to have for dinner. It's like we've fallen into this routine where we exist together but don't really see each other anymore. "I don't know. It's been… a while."

She sighs, leaning back in her chair. "That's not good, Lex. You need to talk to him. Before it's too late."

"Too late?" The words send a jolt through me, and I feel a pit forming in my stomach. "You think it's already over, don't you?"

"No, I don't," she says quickly, shaking her head. "But I do think if you don't deal with this now, it's going to fester. And that's when things really start falling apart."

I nod, knowing she's right. But the thought of actually confronting Jeremy, of asking him if there's more going on than just work stress, makes me feel like I'm standing on the edge of a cliff. One wrong move, and everything could come crashing down.

She gives me a sympathetic smile. "Take your time, but don't wait too long. You deserve answers, Lex. And you deserve peace."

After we finish our coffees, we part ways with promises to check in later. But as I walk back to my car, the weight of our conversation lingers. I keep replaying it in my head, wondering if I'm ready to hear whatever he might have to say. What if he's not the man I thought he was? What if this entire marriage has been built on something fragile, something that could break at any moment?

Or, what if I'm just so lost and insecure from this relationship that I ruin it by asking if there is something else. Someone else…

Back home, I stand in the middle of my office, staring at the blank canvas sitting in the corner. I've been trying to throw myself into my art. Sometimes it works and I'm able to draw. And sometimes, it doesn't. I'm so focused on how we are doing that I can't even create.

I sigh, picking up a paintbrush and dip it into some paint, my mind whirling with thoughts I can't quite put into words. The brush strokes are messy, reflecting the jumble of emotions inside me.

I'm angry. I'm scared. I'm lost.

The painting is abstract, a swirl of colors that don't really make sense together but somehow convey exactly what I'm feeling. As the hours pass, I lose myself, each stroke of the brush pulling me further away from reality.

When the painting is done, I step back and examine it. It's not my best work, but it's raw, and in some strange way, it feels like a reflection of my life right now. Chaotic. Uncertain. On the verge of something breaking.

I wipe my hands on an old rag and sit down on the floor, staring up at the painting. It's strange how something so abstract can feel so personal.

Chapter Seven

I pull my phone from my pocket, checking it again for any sign of a message. Nothing. My fingers hover over the screen as I debate sending another text. He's late. Maybe he got held up with a power line. But it's been over an hour now.

I glance at the clock, then at the table, where two plates sit ready, food steaming and untouched. The sound of the oven timer ticking echoes in the quiet, making the room feel more empty than it should.

I've been looking forward to tonight all week, planning every detail down to the wine I knew Jeremy liked—something light, something that wouldn't feel heavy after a long day at work.

I walk over to the table, adjusting the napkins out of habit, trying to shake off the creeping frustration. We used to do this all the time, quiet nights at home, just the two of us, talking about anything and everything. But now, moments like these feel rare.

The door creaks open, and I hear his keys hit the counter. My heart jumps, and I turn, ready with a smile. But it falters when I see him.

He looks exhausted. Dark circles hang under his eyes, and his shoulders slump as he shrugs off his coat, tossing it carelessly onto a chair. "Hey," he mutters, rubbing his face as he walks into the kitchen.

"Hey," I whisper, trying to keep my voice steady. "I was starting to wonder if you were coming home."

He looks at the table, his eyes flicking over the candles and the plates. No Smile. No raised brow. No reaction what-so-ever. "Sorry," he says, "I'm not really hungry. I had to grab something quick right before fixing a power line."

I bite the inside of my cheek, nodding even though my throat feels tight. I spent hours preparing dinner, hoping it might be a chance for us to reconnect, but now it feels like all that effort was for nothing. "It's fine," I say, though it isn't.

He sighs while running a hand through his hair. "I'm just… I'm exhausted, Lex. Work's been a nightmare lately."

"I get it." I reply, though the words taste bitter.

He doesn't respond, just sinks into the chair like he's carrying the weight of the world. I sit across from him, the candles flickering between us. I want to reach out, to hold his hand, to tell him that I'm here, that we can figure this out together. But there's this invisible wall between us and I don't know how to break through it.

"So… how was your day?" I ask, trying to sound casual, as if tonight wasn't supposed to be special.

He shrugs, his eyes on the floor. "Long. Stressful. The usual."

I nod, watching him, waiting for him to say more. But the silence stretches out, heavy and uncomfortable, until I can't take it anymore.

"I just thought… Maybe tonight we could spend some time together," I say, my voice soft. "Like we used to."

He looks up, "I know. I don't have it in me tonight."

The disappointment hits me hard, like a punch to the gut. But I swallow it down, forcing a smile. "It's okay," I say, though it's not. "Maybe another time."

Jeremy stands, stretching his arms over his head. "Yeah. Another time."

As he walks toward the bedroom, I sit there, staring at the untouched food.

I blow out the candles and start clearing the table, forcing my tears back. I've been trying so hard to be patient, to be understanding, but it feels like every time I reach out, he pulls further away.

When I finish, I follow him into the bedroom, the tension still sitting heavy in my chest. He's already lying in bed, scrolling through his phone like nothing happened. The sight of him there, so distant even when we're just feet apart, makes my heart sink. I slip under the covers beside him, careful not to disturb his quiet bubble of exhaustion, but the silence between us feels unbearable.

For a moment, I think about just turning over and going to sleep, burying the questions swirling in my head. But I can't. Not tonight.

"Jeremy?" I ask softly, not looking at him. My fingers twist in the blanket, bracing for whatever comes next. "Is there… someone else?"

The words hang in the air like a loaded gun, the silence stretching out until I finally turn my head to look at him.

He frowns, lowering his phone as he processes what I just asked. "What? No. Why would you even think that?" His voice isn't angry, just confused, but it still makes me feel small.

I bite my lip, hating that I even asked, but I can't help it. "You've been so distant, and I don't know… I guess I just…"

He sighs, setting his phone down on the nightstand and turning toward me. His eyes soften, and for the first time in what feels like weeks, I see the man I know—my Jeremy. "Baby, there's no one else. I promise. It's just work. I'm exhausted all the time, but it's nothing to do with you."

I want to believe him, and maybe that's enough for now. I nod, blinking back the sting in my eyes. "It just feels like you're slipping away from me."

He shifts closer, his hand reaching out to touch my cheek, gently brushing away the tear that's forming. "I'm sorry. I don't want to make you feel like that."

The warmth of his hand against my skin makes my chest tighten. But this time it's not from frustration—it's from hope. Maybe things aren't as far gone as I thought. Maybe we're not as broken as we feel.

He pulls me closer, wrapping his arm around me, and for the first time in weeks, I let myself lean into him, letting the steady beat of his heart calm my own racing thoughts. I close my eyes, feeling the weight of his arms around me.

"I love you," I whisper, my voice barely audible against his chest. I'm not sure if he hears me at first, but then he presses a kiss to the top of my head, his lips lingering just a little longer than usual.

"I love you too," he murmurs. "I know I haven't been showing it, but I do."

We stay like that for a while, wrapped up in each other, and for the first time in what feels like forever, the silence between us feels comfortable. The exhaustion is still there; the problems aren't magically solved, but for now, this is enough.

Maybe tomorrow will be different. Maybe it won't. But at least for tonight, I can breathe.

It's Sunday afternoon, and for once, the house doesn't feel empty. Jeremy sits beside me on the couch, his presence both comforting and nerve-wracking.

"I know work's been crazy for you, but I miss us. What if we made a plan? On days you're home by seven, we could have dinner together, talk a bit before bed?"

He's quiet for a moment, and I can almost see the gears turning in his head. "That could work," he says slowly. "And on weekends, when I'm not working, we could do something together? I know I've been on the game a lot…"

A small spark of hope ignites in my chest. "Really? That would be great."

He nods, a small smile tugging at the corners of his mouth. "Yeah, I'd like that. I know things have been… off lately."

I reach out, taking his hand in mine. It feels warm, familiar. "I just want us to be us again," I say softly.

He squeezes my hand, and for the first time in weeks, I feel like we're on the same page. "Me too, Lex. Me too."

We spend the rest of the afternoon on the couch, scrolling through tv for something to watch. It feels almost normal, and my shoulders don't feel so tense.

"Oh, how about this one?" I say, pointing to a cheesy rom-com.

He groans playfully. "Really? You know I can't stand those."

I stick my tongue out at him. "Come on, it'll be fun. I promise I won't make you watch another one for at least a month."

He raises an eyebrow. "A whole month? I doubt it."

I roll my eyes, letting out a laugh.

As the movie starts, I snuggle closer to him, relishing the feeling of his arm around me. It's been so long since we've done this, just existing together without the weight of the world on us.

Halfway through the movie, he shifts beside me.

"Hey, I'm gonna use the bathroom real quick,"

I nod, pausing the movie. "Want me to wait for you?"

"Nah, go ahead. I might be awhile. Stomach's been acting up again."

As he disappears down the hall, I can't help but worry. He's been complaining about stomach issues for weeks now, but he keeps brushing off my suggestions to see a doctor. Maybe it's time I take matters into my own hands. I make a mental note to look up some healthier recipes. A change in our diet might help, and honestly, it couldn't hurt either of us.

The minutes tick by, and I glance at the clock more frequently. He's been in the bathroom for almost an hour now. I try to focus on the movie, but my mind keeps wandering, worry gnawing at the edges of my thoughts.

Just as I'm about to get up and check on him, I hear the bathroom door open. Jeremy shuffles back into the living room, looking a bit pale but offering a weak smile.

"Sorry about that," he mumbles, sinking back onto the couch beside me. "Told you it might be awhile."

I bite my lip, debating whether to push the issue. "Are you sure you don't want to see a doctor? This has been going on for weeks now."

He shakes his head, waving off my concern. "It's fine, Lex. Probably just stress or something I ate. It'll pass."

I'm not convinced, but I let it go for now. We've made progress today, and I don't want to ruin it by nagging. Instead, I lean into him, breathing in his familiar scent. "If you're sure,"

We finish the movie in comfortable silence, and as the credits roll, I realize how late it's gotten. The sky outside has darkened, and a quick glance at my phone shows its past 9 PM.

"We should probably think about dinner," I say, stretching as I stand up.

He yawns, looking more relaxed than he has in days. "Actually, I'm not really hungry. That stomach thing, you know?"

I nod, understanding. "How about we just call it a night then? We can curl up in bed?"

He smiles, and it reaches his eyes this time. "That sounds perfect."

We make our way to the bedroom, the routine of getting ready for bed feeling both familiar and somehow new. As I slip under the covers, he wraps an arm around me, pulling me close.

"This was nice," he whispers into my hair. "I've missed this. Missed you."

I feel tears prick at the corners of my eyes, but I blink them back. "I've missed you too," I manage to say, my voice barely above a whisper.

We lay there in the darkness, the sound of our breathing the only noise in the room. I can feel his heartbeat against my back, steady and reassuring. For the first time in weeks, maybe even months, I feel truly at peace.

As I drift off, I can't help but think about the day. We're talking again, really talking, and spending time together which is what we need.

Maybe from here, things will get better. We'll stick to our new plan, make time for each other, and slowly rebuild what we've lost. It won't be easy, I know that. There will be setbacks and arguments, days when it feels like we're right back where we started. But today has given me hope.

I snuggle closer to him, feeling his arm tighten around me in response.

Chapter Eight

The warmth of his hand on mine lingers even after we've finished dinner and cleared the table. There's a fragile hope blooming in my chest, but I'm afraid to nurture it too much. We've been here before, teetering on the edge of reconnection, only to fall back into our old patterns.

I lean against the kitchen counter, watching him as he loads the dishwasher.

"I was thinking," I start, my voice sounding too loud in the quiet kitchen, "maybe we could do something this weekend?"

He pauses, a plate hovering halfway to the rack. "This weekend?" He frowns slightly, and I feel my heart sink. "I promised the guys I'd help with a project on Saturday, but Sunday could work."

I nod, "Sunday sounds good. Any ideas on what you'd like to do?"

He shrugs, resuming his task. "We could go for a hike, maybe?"

The suggestion surprises me. We haven't been hiking in years, not since before his new job, before everything changed. "That… that sounds really nice, actually."

He gives me a small smile, and for a moment, I see a glimmer of the boy I fell in love with. "It's a date, then."

The phrase sends a flutter through my stomach. A date. When was the last time we actually went on a date?

As he finishes with the dishes, I find myself drifting to the living room. My gaze falls on the bookshelf, filled with photo albums I haven't looked at in ages. On impulse, I pull out our wedding album.

I settle onto the couch, the weight of the album heavy in my lap. As I open it, the smell of old paper and memories wafts up. The first photo is of us, fresh-faced and grinning, cutting the cake. We look so young, so full of hope and promise.

"What've you got there?" Jeremy's voice startles me. I look up to see him leaning against the doorframe, his expression curious.

"Our wedding album," I say, patting the space next to me. "Want to take a trip down memory lane?"

He hesitates for a moment, but then he crosses the room and sits beside me, close enough that I can feel the warmth radiating from his body.

We flip through the pages together, laughing at the outdated hairstyles of our friends, reminiscing about the little details we'd almost forgotten. When we get to a photo of our first dance, I feel him tense beside me.

"God, I was so nervous," he says."I was sure I was going to step on your dress and rip it."

I laugh softly. "I remember. You kept looking at your feet."

"Yeah, well, I didn't want to mess up the most important dance of my life."

The sincerity in his voice makes me look up at him. Our eyes meet, and for a moment, it's like no time has passed at all. We're those two kids again, madly in love and ready to take on the world together.

I lean in and kiss him. It's soft, tentative, nothing like the passionate kisses we used to share. But it's something. A spark in the darkness. I haven't felt confident lately. Kissing him out of thin air or thinking about it felt like a crime. He'd just leave the room after a kiss and I eventually would give up trying.

When I pull back, his eyes are wide with surprise. "Lex…" he starts, but trails off, seemingly at a loss for words.

"I'm sorry," I say quickly, embarrassment flooding through me. "I shouldn't have—"

But before I can finish, his hand is on my cheek, drawing me back in for another kiss. This one is deeper, filled with all the words we haven't been able to say to each other.

When we finally break apart, we're both breathless. Jeremy rests his forehead against mine, his eyes closed. "I've missed you," he whispers. "So much."

Tears prick at my eyes. "I've missed you too."

"We should go out this Sunday, for dinner."

"Really?" My heart flutters.

"Yes, really."

We stay like that for a long moment, just breathing each other in. It feels like a turning point, like maybe we've finally found our way back to each other.

But as he pulls away, I see a flicker of something in his eyes. Guilt? Uncertainty? Before I can decipher it, it's gone, replaced by a soft smile.

"It's getting late," he says, glancing at the clock. "We should probably turn in."

I nod, trying to ignore the nagging feeling in the pit of my stomach. "Yeah, you're right."

As we get ready for bed, moving around each other in a dance we've perfected over years, I can't shake the feeling that something's still off. He seems distracted, his movements almost mechanical.

We climb into bed, and he turns off the lamp on his nightstand. In the darkness, I reach for his hand. He takes it, giving it a gentle squeeze, but there's a hesitancy to the gesture that wasn't there earlier.

"Goodnight, Lex," he murmurs.

"Goodnight," I reply, staring up at the ceiling.

As his breathing evens out beside me, signaling he's fallen asleep, I'm left wide awake. The evening replays in my mind, the dinner, the kisses, the moment of connection. It felt real. It felt like us again…kind of.

But now, in the night's quiet, doubts creep in. Was it real? Or just a momentary reprieve from the distance that's grown between us? And that look in his eyes. What was he not telling me?

I turn onto my side, watching the rise and fall of Jeremy's chest in the dim light filtering through the curtains. I want so badly to believe that we're on the right track and that we can find our way back to each other. But as sleep finally claims me, one thought echoes in my mind:

One step forward, two steps back.

Chapter Nine

I watch him as he studies the menu, his brow furrowed in concentration. It's been so long since we've done this—dressed up, gone out, just the two of us. The weight of expectations sits heavily on my shoulders.

"What are you thinking of getting?" I ask, desperate to break the silence that's settled between us.

He looks up, a small smile tugging at the corners of his mouth. "Probably the chicken parm. You know me, creature of habit."

I nod, returning his smile. "Some things never change."

The familiarity of it all—his predictable order, the way he absently fiddles with his napkin—sends a pang through my chest. It's comforting and painful all at once, a reminder of what we once were and what we're struggling to be again.

Our waiter appears, a young man with a cheerful demeanor that feels almost out of place in our bubble of tentative reconnection. We place our orders, and as he walks away, I reach for my water glass, needing something to do with my hands.

"So," he starts, clearing his throat. "How's your art coming along? You mentioned you were working on some new pieces."

The question catches me off guard. It's been months since he's asked about my work. "It's… going well." I didn't want to tell him I've been struggling with my art.

He nods, seeming genuinely interested. "That's great, Lex. I noticed you've not been in your office lately and was kind of worried."

Using my nickname, so casual and intimate, makes my heart skip a beat. But what he doesn't realize is I haven't been in there much because our relationship has been draining down the toilet for a year.

As he opens his mouth to respond, a familiar voice cuts through the restaurant's ambient noise.

"Alexis? Jeremy? What a surprise!"

I turn to see Lilly approaching our table, Zeke in tow. My stomach drops. This was supposed to be our night, a chance to reconnect without any outside interference. But here's Lilly, beaming at us like she's stumbled upon a delightful surprise.

"Lilly, Zeke, hi," I manage, forcing a smile. "What brings you here?"

"Oh, just a little date night," Lilly says, waving her hand dismissively. "Mind if we join you for a minute?"

Before either Jeremy or I can respond, Lilly's pulling up a chair, Zeke following suit with an apologetic shrug.

"So, tell me everything," Lilly says, leaning in conspiratorially. "How's life at home? Are you two still doing that dinner thing you talked about?"

I feel Jeremy tense beside me, his posture stiffening. "We're working on it," he says, his voice tight.

Her eyes narrow slightly, darting between us. "And how about your weekends? Any fun plans coming up?"

The rapid-fire questions feel like an interrogation. I glance at Jeremy, seeing the same discomfort I feel reflected in his eyes.

"We're taking things day by day," I say, trying to keep my tone light. "Actually, we were thinking of going for a hike next sunday."

"A hike?" Lilly's eyebrows shoot up. "That's... different for you two."

I feel a flash of irritation at her surprise. "We used to hike all the time," I say, perhaps a bit more defensively than necessary.

An awkward silence falls over the table. I can see Jeremy retreating into himself, his gaze fixed on the tablecloth. Zeke, bless him, seems to sense the tension.

"Well, we should let you two enjoy your dinner," he says, standing up. "It was great running into you."

Lilly looks like she wants to protest, but Zeke's hand on her shoulder seems to make her think better of it. "Right, of course. Enjoy your evening!"

As they walk away, I let out a sigh. I turn to Jeremy, ready to laugh off the awkward encounter, but the words die in my throat. His expression is closed off, distant in a way that's become all too familiar lately.

"Jeremy?" I reach out, my fingers brushing against his hand. He pulls away, almost imperceptibly, but the small movement feels like a chasm opening between us.

"I'm fine," he says, not meeting my eyes. "Just… not very hungry anymore."

The rest of the dinner passes in a haze of stilted conversation and long silences. By the time we're in the car, heading home, the tentative hope I'd felt earlier has all but evaporated.

He stares straight ahead as he drives, his knuckles white on the steering wheel. I want to reach out, to bridge this sudden gap between us, but something holds me back. The silence in the car is oppressive, filled with all the things we're not saying.

As we pull into our driveway, I can't take it anymore. "Talk to me. What's going on?"

He sighs, running a hand through his hair. "Nothing. I'm just tired."

"Bullshit," I say, surprising myself with the vehemence in my voice. "This isn't about being tired. What happened back there?"

His jaw clenches. "Can we not do this right now? Please?"

The plea in his voice makes me pause. I study his profile in the dim light of the car, seeing the exhaustion etched in the lines of his face. Whatever's going on, pushing him now won't help.

"Okay," I say softly. "But we need to talk about this. Soon."

He nods, a quick, jerky motion, before getting out of the car. I follow him into the house, watching as he heads straight for the bedroom without another word.

As I hear the bedroom door close, I'm left standing in our living room, surrounded by the echoes of our failed date night. The house feels colder somehow, emptier. I wrap my arms around myself.

One step forward, two steps back. The phrase echoes in my mind as I sink onto the couch, the weight of disappointment settling heavy on my shoulders. As I stare at the closed bedroom door, I can't help but wonder if we're fighting for something that's already lost.

THE BRUSH GLIDES ACROSS THE CANVAS, LEAVING A streak of crimson in its wake. I step back, squinting at the painting before me. It's abstract, a swirl of dark colors punctuated by bursts of fiery reds and oranges. I'm not sure what it means, but it feels right. It feels like the chaos in my head made visible.

I've been painting for hours, losing myself in the rhythmic strokes and the pungent smell of oil paints. The sun has long since set, and the only light in my office comes from the harsh glow of the overhead lamp. My back aches from standing so long, but I can't bring myself to stop. Not yet.

In the distance, I hear the front door open and close. Jeremy's home. I glance at the clock on the wall and frown. It's past midnight. Again.

I wait for him to call out, to come find me like he used to. But the house remains quiet aside from the soft thud of his footsteps heading straight for the bathroom. The familiar sound of the door closing.

With a sigh, I turn back to my painting.

I don't know what to do anymore. This back-and-forth god knows what bullshit between us is breaking my heart. The idea of parting ways with him sweeps through my thoughts. But I shake my head while I dip my brush in a deep blue, adding depth to the swirling chaos on the canvas. I thought we were making progress, or so I thought. But it feels like we're right back where we started.

The sound of the toilet flushing makes me jump, the brush in my hand making a messy streak. Fuck. I pause, listening. The bathroom door opens, and I hear Jeremy's footsteps again, this time heading towards our bedroom. No detour to me, his office, no goodnight kiss, just straight to the bedroom.

I swallow hard, fighting back the lump forming in my throat. This is becoming our new normal, and I hate it.

Setting down my brush, I wipe my paint-stained hands on my already-stained apron. It's late, but sleep feels impossible right now. Instead, I start cleaning up my brushes.

I rinse the last brush, watching the swirl of colors disappear down the drain.

By the time I make it to our bedroom, he is already asleep, or pretending to be. His back is to my side of the bed, his breathing slow and even. I slip under the covers as quietly as I can, careful not to disturb him.

Lying there in the dark, I stare at the ceiling, my mind racing. What happened to our plans? Our promises to each other? It feels like we're drifting further apart with each passing day, and I don't know how to stop it.

MORNING COMES TOO SOON, THE HARSH LIGHT OF DAWN filtering through the curtains. The bed beside me is empty, the sheets cool to the touch. Jeremy must have left already. Normally I get up with him but he didn't bother to wake me.

I drag myself out of bed, my body protesting after the late night. In the kitchen, I find a hastily scribbled note on the counter:

Early meeting. Don't wait up tonight.

No, I love you, no sweet message. I crumple the note in my fist, anger and frustration bubbling up inside me. This kind of marriage isn't what we promised each other.

Before I can think better of it, I grab my phone and type out a text,

ME

We need to talk. Soon.

I hit send before I can lose my nerve, then toss the phone aside. A thought emerges within me as my eyes rest upon the fruit bowl placed on the counter.

That would be fun to create. I hurry to my office and take out a pencil and begin drawing in my sketchbook.

By the time I step back to survey my work, the sun is high in the sky.

I set down my pencil, flexing my cramped hand. My gaze falls on my phone, sitting silently on the nearby table. Before I can second-guess myself, I grab it and scroll to Lilly's number.

The phone rings once, twice, three times. I'm about to hang up when Lilly's cheerful voice breaks through.

"Lex girl! How are ya?"

I hesitate, unsure how to broach the subject. "I'm… okay. Listen, Lilly, I wanted to talk to you about the other night at Olive Garden."

There's a pause on the other end of the line. When Lilly speaks again, her tone is carefully neutral. "Oh? What about it?"

I take a deep breath, steeling myself. "Your questions… they felt a bit invasive. Jeremy and I were trying to have a quiet dinner, and it just seemed like you were pushing for information."

Lilly's laugh tinkles through the phone, light and dismissive. "I was just being friendly! You know me, always curious about what's going on with my best friend."

Her casual response makes something twist in my gut. "It didn't feel friendly. It felt like an interrogation."

"Girl," Lilly says, her voice taking on a slightly patronizing tone, "I think you might be overreacting a bit. I was just making conversation. If I crossed a line, I'm sorry, but it really wasn't a big deal."

I close my eyes, feeling a headache building behind my temples. "Maybe not to you, but it upset Jeremy. He's been even more distant since that night."

"Well, that sounds like a Jeremy problem, not a

me problem," Lilly replies, a hint of impatience creeping into her voice. "Have you considered that maybe he's just stressed from work?"

Her words hit a little too close to home, echoing the excuses I've been making for Jeremy's behavior.

"That's not the point, Lilly. I'm trying to tell you that your actions had consequences."

"Look, Alexis," Lilly says with a sigh, "I appreciate you calling, but I think you're making a mountain out of a molehill here. It was just a dinner conversation. If Jeremy can't handle a few innocent questions, maybe there are bigger issues you two need to address."

Her dismissal stings, leaving me feeling small and foolish. "Right," I say, my voice tight. "Well, I should go. I've got… things to do."

"Alright, hon. Take care. And try not to stress so much, okay? It's not good for you."

The call ends, leaving me feeling more alone than ever. I stare at my phone, a mix of anger and hurt swirling in my chest. Is Lilly right? Am I overreacting? Or is she brushing off my concerns too easily?

I turn back to my sketch, and figure out what colors and what else to add to it.

Chapter Ten

My phone sits silent on the kitchen counter, mocking me with its blank screen. It's been three hours since I texted Jeremy about needing to talk. Three hours of silence that speak volumes.

I pour myself another cup of coffee, though my hands are already jittery from the previous two. The fruit bowl still sits on the counter, half-finished in my sketchbook, waiting for colors that I can't seem to choose. Everything feels wrong today–the light, the silence, even the air feels thick with unspoken words.

The sound of a car door slamming outside makes me jump. Through the kitchen window, I watch as Jeremy walks up our driveway, his orange work shirt bright against the grey afternoon sky. He's home early. My heart pounds against my ribs as I hear his key in the lock.

"Hey," he says, dropping his lunch box on the

counter. His eyes meet mine for a moment before darting away. "Got your text."

I grip my coffee mug tighter, anchoring myself. "Yeah, I thought we should talk about what happened at dinner."

He sighs, running a hand through his hair. "Look, I'm sorry if I ruined our night out. I just... I wasn't expecting to run into them."

"It wasn't about running into them," I say, my voice quieter than I intended. "It was about how you completely shut down afterward. You've been distant ever since, more than usual."

"More than usual?" His tone sharpens. "What's that supposed to mean?"

"You know exactly what it means, Jeremy." The words come out in a rush now, months of bottled emotions spilling over. "You're never really here anymore. Even when you're home, you're somewhere else. The bathroom, the bedroom, anywhere but with me."

He leans against the counter, creating more distance between us. "I told you, work's been—"

"Stop." The word comes out harder than I meant it to. "Please, just... stop with the work excuse. I know your job is demanding, but this is different. You're different."

Silence fills the kitchen. Outside, a neighbor's dog barks, the sound muffled and far away. Jeremy stares at the floor, his jaw clenched tight.

"What do you want me to say, Alexis?"

The use of my full name stings. He only calls me Alexis when he's angry or pulling away. "I want you to tell me the truth. What's really going on?"

He pushes away from the counter, pacing the small space of our kitchen. "Nothing's going on. I'm just tired. Tired of the pressure, tired of feeling like I'm not enough, tired of—" He pauses, as if catching himself.

"Tired of what?" I press, my heart hammering. "Tired of us?"

The question hangs in the air between us, heavy with possibility. Jeremy's shoulders slump, and when he finally looks at me, I see something in his eyes that breaks my heart–resignation.

"Maybe," he whispers. "Maybe I am."

The coffee mug slips from my grasp, shattering against the tile floor. Dark liquid spreads across the white ceramic, like blood from a wound. Neither of us moves to clean it up.

"How long?" My voice sounds strange to my own ears, distant and hollow. "How long have you felt this way?"

He shakes his head, not meeting my eyes. "I don't know. It's not like I woke up one morning and everything was different. It just... happened. Little by little."

I wrap my arms around myself, suddenly cold despite the warm afternoon. "Do you still love me?"

"Of course I do." The words come quickly, automatically, but they lack the conviction they once held. "I just don't know if that's enough anymore."

Tears blur my vision, but I refuse to let them fall. Not yet. Not while I still have words that need saying. "I've been trying so hard, Jeremy. Making your lunches, keeping the house clean, trying to plan dates, trying to make you happy…"

"I never asked you to do any of that," he cuts in, frustration edging his voice.

"No, you didn't. But I did it because I love you. Because I've been fighting for us while you've been… what? Just going through the motions?"

He runs both hands through his hair, a gesture so familiar it makes my chest ache. "That's not fair."

"None of this is fair." My voice cracks. "We promised each other forever, and now you're standing there telling me you're tired of us?"

The silence that follows is deafening. Outside, life goes on–cars pass, birds chirp, the neighbor's dog continues to bark. But in our kitchen, time seems to stand still.

Finally, Jeremy speaks, his voice barely above a whisper. "Maybe we need some time apart."

The words hit me like a physical blow. "Time apart," I repeat, tasting the bitterness of the phrase. "You mean a separation?"

He nods slowly. "Just to figure things out. To see if…" He trails off, but I hear the unspoken words, anyway. To see if we still work. To see if we're worth saving.

I look around our kitchen–at the broken mug on the floor, the half-empty coffeepot, the fruit bowl I'd been sketching. All these ordinary things that suddenly feel extraordinary in their finality. This could be the last time we stand here together as husband and wife.

"Okay," I say, surprising us both. "If that's what you want."

He looks up sharply, perhaps expecting more of a fight. But I'm tired too. Tired of being the only one trying, tired of watching us drift further apart, tired of pretending everything's fine when we're clearly broken.

"I'll stay at my brother's," he says after a moment. "I can pack some things tonight."

I nod, not trusting myself to speak. He moves past me toward our bedroom, and I hear him pulling out a duffel bag, opening drawers. Each sound is another crack in my heart.

Standing alone in the kitchen, I finally let the tears fall, mixing with the spilled coffee at my feet. One thought echoes in my mind, over and over: This is how a marriage ends–not with a bang, but with quiet words on a Tuesday afternoon, and coffee spreading across a kitchen floor.

Chapter Eleven

The house feels different at night now. Every creak, every shadow holds a memory of him. I lie awake in our bed—my bed now—staring at the ceiling fan as it spins lazy circles above me. The space beside me feels infinite.

It's been three days since he left. Three days of existing in this strange limbo where everything looks the same but feels completely different. His toothbrush is still in the bathroom. His favorite coffee mug still sits in the cabinet. Little pieces of him scattered everywhere, like landmines waiting to explode my heart all over again.

My phone buzzes on the nightstand, making me jump. It's Lilly.

LILLY

Just checking in. You okay?

I stare at the message, unsure how to respond. Am I okay? I don't even know what okay means anymore.

ME

Can't sleep.

LILLY

Want company? I can be there in 15.

It's nearly midnight, and I know she has work tomorrow. But the thought of spending another night alone in this too-quiet house makes my chest tight.

ME

No it's okay.

LILLY:

Already putting my shoes on.

Fifteen minutes later, she's at my door in pajama pants and an oversized sweater, holding a grocery bag. "I brought ice cream," she announces, sweeping past me into the kitchen. "And those chocolate cookies you like from that bakery near my house."

"Lil, you didn't have to do this."

"Yes, I did." She opens cabinets, pulling out bowls with the familiarity of someone who's spent countless hours in this kitchen. "Because that's what best friends do. They show up with sugar and carbs when their person is hurting."

I watch as she scoops generous portions of mint

chocolate chip ice cream into bowls, adding cookies to the side. "Come on," she says, handing me a bowl. "Let's go sit."

We settle on the couch, and I pull the throw blanket over both our laps.

"Want to talk about it?" she asks softly, tucking her feet under her.

I take a bite of ice cream, letting the cold numb my tongue. "I don't even know where to start."

"Start anywhere. Start with right now."

I stare into my bowl, watching the ice cream slowly melt. "Right now… right now, I keep thinking about stupid things. Like how I still make enough coffee for two people every morning. Or how I reach for his hand when I'm watching TV. Or how I…" My voice cracks. "How I still whisper 'good night' to his side of the bed, even though I know he's not there."

Lilly sets her bowl down and pulls me into a hug. The dam breaks, and suddenly I'm sobbing into her shoulder, ice cream forgotten on the coffee table.

"I don't know who I am without him, Lil," I choke out between sobs. "We've been together since high school. He's all I know."

"That's not true," she says firmly, pulling back to look at me. "You're Alexis Kline. You're an artist. You're my best friend. You're the person who helped me through my breakup with Dave, remember? You're the one who organized that fundraiser for the animal shelter last year. You're so many things that have nothing to do with being Jeremy's wife."

I wipe my eyes with the back of my hand. "Then why do I feel so lost?"

"Because change is scary. Because endings hurt. Because you're human." She squeezes my hand. "But you're not alone, okay? I'm right here."

We sit in silence for a while, the ice cream melting forgotten. Outside, a car passes by, its headlights sweeping across the living room walls. I remember how Jeremy and I used to make shadow puppets in those lights, laughing like kids.

"He left his shirts,"

"What?"

"In the closet. He packed some clothes, but he left all his work shirts. The orange ones." I laugh, but it comes out more like a sob. "I keep staring at them every time I open the closet, wondering if he'll come back for them or if I'm supposed to pack them up or…"

"Oh, honey." She pulls me close again. "You don't have to figure that out right now. You don't have to figure anything out right now."

But I do. I have to figure out how to sleep alone, how to cook for one, how to exist in this house full of memories without drowning in them. I have to figure out who I am when I'm not part of "Jeremy and Alexis."

"You know what you need?" she says, sitting up straight. "Your art room. When's the last time you really painted?"

I think back. "Before… everything. I tried sketching that fruit bowl the other day, but…"

"Then that's what we're going to do. Right now."

I blink at her. "It's almost one in the morning."

"So? Van Gogh did some of his best work at night." She's already standing, pulling me up with her. "Come on. You need to get these feelings out somehow, and ice cream can only do so much."

She practically drags me to my art room, flipping on lights as we go. The room looks exactly as I left it days ago–the fruit bowl sketch abandoned on the desk, brushes soaking in murky water, canvas covered in half-formed ideas.

"Clean canvas," she demands, already rummaging through my supplies. "Fresh start."

I want to protest that I'm too tired, too sad, too everything to paint right now. But then she hands me a brush, and something shifts inside me. The weight in my chest doesn't disappear, but it changes, becomes something I might work with.

"I'll stay right here," she says, settling into the old armchair in the corner. "Paint whatever you need to paint. I brought snacks, remember?"

The canvas stares at me, blank and full of possibility. I dip my brush in paint–deep blue, the color of midnight and secrets and change–and begin.

Hours pass. Lilly dozes in the chair, occasionally waking to make encouraging noises or offer commentary. The sky outside gradually lightens from black to grey to pink. And I paint.

I paint the darkness and the light, the endings and the beginnings. I paint my fear and my hope, my grief and my anger. I paint until my arms ache and my eyes burn, until the canvas is a riot of colors and emotions I didn't even know I was holding inside.

When I finally step back, the sun is fully up, casting golden light through the windows. Lilly stirs in her chair, stretching.

"Oh," she breathes, looking at the canvas. "Lex…"

I see my pain laid bare in broad strokes and bold colors. But there's something else there too, something I didn't expect to find. In the chaos of dark blues and angry reds, there are spots of light breaking through–small but persistent, like stars in a storm.

"I think," I say slowly, "I need to paint more."

She smiles, reaching for my hand. "Then that's what we'll do. Whenever you need to, day or night, just call me. I'll be here with snacks and moral support."

I squeeze her hand, grateful beyond words for this friend who shows up at midnight with ice cream and doesn't leave until sunrise. Maybe she's right–maybe I am more than just Jeremy's wife. Maybe it's time to find out who else I can be.

"Thank you," I whisper.

She bumps her shoulder against mine. "Always. Now, how do you feel about breakfast? I make a mean hangover omelet, and emotional hangovers totally count."

For the first time in days, I feel something like a smile tugging at my lips. It's small and fragile, but it's there. Like those spots of light in my painting, breaking through the darkness, promising that maybe, just maybe, there's something waiting on the other side of all this pain.

Chapter Twelve

Two weeks into the separation, and I've developed a routine. Wake up, forget he's gone, remember, cry in the shower, paint until my arms ache, then let Lilly drag me out of the house for something she deems necessary for my "healing." Today, it's shopping.

"You need new clothes," she announces, pulling me through the mall entrance. "Something that makes you feel you again."

"I have clothes," I protest, but let her guide me, anyway. The truth is, getting out of the house helps. It's easier to breathe in public spaces where Jeremy and I never built memories.

"You have sad clothes," she corrects. "We're getting you something that makes you feel strong."

The fluorescent lights of the department store make my head spin a little. Or maybe it's the lack of breakfast–I couldn't stomach anything this morning, the mere thought of food making me queasy. I've been off lately, probably stress.

"Here," she throws me a deep green dress at me. "This would look amazing with your eyes."

I take the dress, running my fingers over the soft fabric. "Where would I even wear this?"

"Anywhere you want. You need to remember who you are outside of…" she trails off, careful not to say his name.

The dressing room is small and warm, mirrors on all sides reflecting my tired face back at me. I slip the dress over my head, surprised by how well it fits. The fabric hugs my curves in a way that feels both comfortable and confident.

"Let me see!"

When I open the door, her face lights up. "Lex, you look incredible."

I turn to the mirror again, really looking this time. The woman staring back at me looks different somehow–stronger maybe, or at least like someone who could be strong. But as I study my reflection, a wave of dizziness hits me. The room tilts slightly, and I grab the doorframe to steady myself.

"Whoa," her hand is on my arm instantly. "You okay?"

"Yeah, just got dizzy for a second."

Her brow furrows with concern. "When's the last time you ate?"

I think back, trying to remember. The days have blurred together. "I don't know."

"That's it. We're getting food right now." She helps me change back into my clothes, insisting on buying the dress despite my protests. "You can't survive on coffee and sadness, Lex."

We make our way to the food court, but the smell of greasy fast food makes my stomach turn. I opt for a smoothie instead, sipping it slowly while Lilly devours a burger.

"Maybe we should get away for a few days," she suggests between bites. "My parents still have that beach house. It would do you good to get out of town."

The idea of leaving, even briefly, makes my chest tight. "I don't know…"

"Just think about it," she says, not pushing further.

Back home, I hang the new dress in my closet, trying not to look at Jeremy's shirts still hanging on his side. The separation was supposed to give us time to figure things out, but all it's done is make everything feel more final.

I'm about to head to my art room when the doorbell rings. My heart jumps–Jeremy still has his key. He wouldn't need to ring. Through the peephole, I see a man in a suit holding an envelope.

My hands shake as I open the door.

"Alexis Kline?" he asks, consulting his clipboard.

I nod, unable to find my voice.

"You've been served." He hands me the envelope

and turns to leave, just like that. Like he hasn't just handed me the end of my marriage in a manila envelope.

I stand in the doorway, opening it. Petition for Divorce. The words blur as tears fill my eyes.

My phone buzzes in my pocket–Lilly, checking in like she always does after we part ways. I can't answer. Can't move. Can't breathe.

I slide down against the wall; the papers clutched to my chest. This is really happening. After five years of marriage, after all our promises and plans, it ends with a stranger at my door and legal documents.

IT'S BEEN A FEW WEEKS SINCE I'VE BEEN SERVED DIVORCE papers. For twenty minutes, I've been in my car observing people go into the brick building that is home to the law offices. Each person who walks through those glass doors is living their own story. Divorce. Custody. Wills. How many hearts have been broken in that building?

My hands won't stop shaking and I grip the steering wheel tighter, trying to steady them, but my whole body feels like it might shatter. The coffee I forced down earlier churns in my stomach.

"You can do this," I whisper to my reflection in

the rearview mirror. I haven't slept more than a few hours at a time since the papers were served. I haven't even taken my ring off yet. My phone buzzes, a text from Lilly.

LILLY

You've got this. Call me after.
Love you.

10:50 AM. My appointment's at 11:00. I can't put this off any longer.

The walk from my car to the building takes forever. My heels click against the pavement–I dressed up for this. Like looking put-together on the outside might help me feel less broken on the inside. The new dress I bought yesterday already feels too tight, constricting around my chest.

A young couple passes me, holding hands, laughing about something. I have to stop walking, press my hand against the rough brick wall until the wave of nausea passes. Was that us once? Young and in love, thinking we had forever?

The elevator smells like someone's too-strong perfume. I watch the numbers climb: 1... 2... 3... My heart pounds harder with each floor. Fourth floor. Jefferson & Associates, Family Law.

The receptionist looks up as I enter, her smile practiced and professional. "Name?"

"Alexis Kline," My voice cracks. "I'm here to... for the..." I can't say it.

"The 11:00 AM with Mr. Kline? Your husband is

already here." Husband. Soon-to-be-ex-husband. The words tangle in my head.

She gestures to the waiting area, where Jeremy sits staring at his phone. He's wearing the blue button-down I got him for his birthday last year. The sight of it hits me like a punch to the gut.

He looks up as I approach.

"Hey," he whispers.

I sink into a chair across from him, my legs too weak to hold me up anymore. The distance between our chairs feels like miles.

A door opens. "Mr. and Mrs. Kline?"

The walk to the lawyer's office is a blur. Jeremy lets me go first–always the gentleman, even now. Even at the end.

Mr. Davis's office is all dark wood and leather, certificates lining the walls. He gestures for us to sit in the two chairs facing his desk. The leather creaks as I sit, and I focus on that sound, on the feel of the smooth armrests under my fingers, anything to keep from looking at Jeremy.

"I have the final papers here," Davis says, pulling out a thick folder. "We'll go through them page by page."

The next hour is torture. Every paragraph is another nail in the coffin of our marriage. Property division. Bank accounts. Insurance policies. Jeremy's voice is steady as he asks questions about retirement accounts and car titles. How can he be so calm?

My signature looks wrong on each page, shaky. I

have to stop twice, close my eyes, breathe deep. Jeremy's cologne–the same kind he's worn since college–fills my nose with each breath. Another thing I'll have to learn to live without.

"And if you'll initial here," Davis says, pointing to another line. "And here."

Each scratch of pen on paper feels like a cut.

Jeremy signs his portion without hesitation. His hand was steady, sure. When did he become so sure about ending us?

"That's everything," Davis says, gathering the papers. "The divorce will be final once processed by the court. We'll notify you both when it's complete."

Just like that. Five years of marriage ended in an hour of signatures and legal jargon.

Outside, the August air bites at my cheeks. It's barely noon, but it feels like days have passed since I sat in my car this morning. Jeremy stands awkwardly beside me on the sidewalk, hands shoved in his pockets.

"So," he says.

"So," I echo. The wind whips my hair across my face, and I'm grateful for the excuse to brush it away, to hide the trembling of my hands.

Last summer, we'd spent weekends getting the yard together, making it look nice. Being silly and spraying water at one another because of the heat. Now we can barely look at each other.

"I'll have my brother help me get the rest of my

things this weekend," he says. "When you're not home."

I nod, throat too tight for words. He takes a step toward his truck, then pauses.

"Take care of yourself, Lex."

Before I can respond, he's gone, leaving me alone on the sidewalk. My legs give out, and I sink onto a nearby bench, no longer caring who might see me fall apart.

I don't know how long I sit there, watching cars pass, watching lives continue as if the world hasn't just ended.

Two weeks pass in a blur. Lilly practically moves in, filling my empty house with chatter and forced normalcy. She's there the day Jeremy's brother helps him move out the last of his things. She's there when I finally take off my ring.

"We should do something," she announces one evening, sprawled on my couch. "Mark the occasion."

"What, like a divorce party?" The words taste bitter.

"No, like... a new beginning ritual. Something symbolic."

That's how we end up in my backyard at

midnight, burning old photos in a fire pit. Not all of them–I'm not ready for that. Just the duplicates, the ones that hurt too much to look at.

"To new beginnings," she says, raising her wineglass.

I raise mine too, watching the flames consume another memory.

A month after the divorce is final, I wake up and realize I haven't cried in three days. It's a small victory, but I'll take it.

The house feels different now. I've rearranged the furniture, painted the walls, tried to erase the traces of 'us' and replace them with just 'me.' Some days it even works.

"You seem better," she says over coffee one morning. "More like yourself."

Am I? The person staring back at me in the mirror feels like a stranger; I don't even recognize myself anymore. But I'm trying to find out.

I start small. Buy groceries just for me. Learn to cook meals for one. Take walks in the evening instead of sitting in an empty house. The world keeps turning, whether or not I'm ready.

Some nights are still hard. I lie awake, staring at his side of the bed–my side now, I've started sleeping in the middle–wondering if he lies awake too. Wondering if he misses me, misses us. Wondering if I'll ever stop missing him.

But slowly, breath by breath, day by day, I'm learning how to exist in this new reality. Learning how to be Alexis instead of Jeremy-and-Alexis.

Chapter Thirteen

"Lilly, I love you, but you need to go home." I lean against my kitchen counter, watching her arrange leftovers in my fridge for the third time this week. "I'll be okay."

She pauses, a container of pasta suspended midair. "Are you sure? Because I can—"

"I'm sure." I manage a small smile. "You have your own life to live. I need to figure out how to be alone."

She closes the fridge, her face pinched with worry. "Promise you'll call if you need anything?"

"Promise."

After she leaves, the silence settles around me like a heavy blanket. My gaze drifts to my art room door, closed for weeks now. The thought of picking up a brush feels impossible, like trying to speak a language I've forgotten.

I wander through the house, touching things

absently–the throw pillow Jeremy's mom made us for Christmas, the coffee mug with a chip in the rim from when we dropped boxes moving in, the framed photo I still haven't taken down from the hallway. Each object holds a memory, and each memory feels like a paper cut–small but stinging.

I grab my keys instead of dwelling on it all.

The cemetery gates are already radiating heat when I drive through, the metal shimmering in the August sun. Even at nine in the morning, the air feels thick. I park in my usual spot–under the big oak tree where mom's favorite cardinals usually nest, though they're quiet today, probably hiding from the heat.

The grass crunches under my feet, brown and brittle from weeks without rain. I make my way to her headstone, the path so familiar I could walk it blindfolded. Seven years, and it still feels like yesterday.

"Hi, Mom." My voice cracks as I sink down beside her grave, the sun-warmed stone pressing against my back. "I really messed up."

Beads of sweat form at my temples, but I don't move to the shade. The heat feels appropriate somehow–uncomfortable, inescapable, like everything else these days.

"Remember how you always said I rushed into things? That I needed to be sure?" I trace the dates carved in stone with trembling fingers. "You were right. About the marriage, about everything."

My chest feels tight, like I can't get enough of the thick summer air. "I don't know who I am anymore, Mom. I haven't painted in weeks. Can't even open the door to my art room. Everything just feels… empty."

A butterfly lands on a nearby flower–one of the fresh ones someone must have left this morning. Mom loved butterflies. "They remind us that beautiful things can come from hard changes," she used to say. The irony isn't lost on me.

"Seven years," I whisper. "Seven years you've been gone, and I still expect you to answer. To tell me what to do, how to fix this." Tears blur my vision, evaporating almost as quickly as they fall in the August heat. "I need you so much right now."

The air is completely still, heavy with humidity. Mom used to love summer mornings, though. "Everything's more alive in the summer," she'd say, tending to her garden before the real heat set in.

"Jeremy's brother came by yesterday to get the last of his things." My voice sounds hollow, even to my own ears. "Found one of his old t-shirts under the bed. I… I couldn't give it back. How pathetic is that?"

I rest my head against the warm stone, letting the tears come. No one here to see them anyway, just the butterflies and the cicadas and whatever part of Mom might still be listening.

"I keep thinking about our last conversation." The memory rises unbidden–Mom in her hospital bed, her hand so fragile in mine, the heat making the room feel even more suffocating. "You made me promise to be happy, remember? To not let fear hold me back?" A bitter laugh escapes. "Well, I tried. I really did. And look where it got me."

My stomach growls, reminding me I haven't eaten since… yesterday? The days blur together lately. The thought of food makes me slightly queasy.

"I should go," I say, wiping sweat from my forehead. "Need to eat something. You'd be yelling at me right now for skipping meals."

Standing makes my head spin a little. Probably from the heat, or the crying, or the lack of food. I press my hand against the headstone to steady myself.

"I miss you, Mom. So much it hurts sometimes." I touch the stone one last time. "I'll come back soon."

The diner off Main Street blasts cold air conditioning when I walk in, raising goosebumps on my sweaty skin. The bell above the door chimes–the same bell that's been there since I was a kid coming here with Mom after church. Martha, the waitress who's worked here forever, looks up from wiping down the counter.

"Alexis?" Her face softens with concern. "Honey, you look overheated. Sit, sit."

She leads me to a booth by the window, not my usual spot with Jeremy, thank god. The vinyl seat sticks to my legs as I slide in.

"The usual?" she asks, already pouring ice water.

"Yes please."

As she walks away, I catch her whispering with the other waitress, both glancing my way with sympathy. Word travels fast in small towns. Everyone probably knows about the divorce by now.

The ice water helps clear my head a little, and I gulp it down, letting the cold shock my system. Mom used to say that sometimes you need a shock to remind yourself that you're still alive.

BACK HOME, THE HOUSE FEELS BIGGER SOMEHOW. Emptier. Even with the AC running, there's a stuffiness that has nothing to do with the August heat. I try to read but can't focus on the words. Try to watch TV, but every show seems to be about relationships. Finally, I curl up on the couch with a light blanket, flipping through Netflix without really seeing it. Some romantic comedy starts playing–I should probably change it, but I don't have the energy.

My eyes grow heavy as the movie plays on. On screen, a couple fights and makes up, the kind of simple conflict that can be resolved in two hours or less. Real life isn't that neat. Real life is messy and complicated and sometimes there is no making up.

The last thing I remember thinking before sleep takes me is that Mom would know what to do. Mom always knew what to do.

CHAPTER FOURTEEN

The morning light filtering through my bedroom window is too bright, too harsh. I roll over with a groan, my stomach churning. Third morning in a row I've woken up like this. Must be the stress of everything finally catching up with me.

I drag myself out of bed, passing the blank walls where our photos used to hang. The nail holes stare back at me like tiny wounds, reminders of everything we've lost. We had so many plans for this house. That corner in the living room where we were going to put a crib someday. The backyard where Jeremy talked about building a swing set.

The box he dropped off yesterday still sits unopened on the kitchen counter. I make my way around it, like it's a black hole threatening to pull me in. The coffee maker–a wedding gift from his parents–sits quiet and unused. I haven't been able to stomach coffee lately. Even the smell of it sends my stomach rolling.

Instead, I sink into the couch with a glass of water, letting my mind drift to when things started changing. Was it the new job? The long hours spent apart? Or did we just stop trying somewhere along the way?

I remember the night he got the call about the interview at the power company. We were lying in bed, talking about our future like we used to do every night.

His eyes lit up when he told me about the salary, the benefits.

"If you get this job," I'd told him, curled against his chest, "we could start saving for a family."

He'd smiled then, that bright, hopeful smile I fell in love with in high school. "Our own little soccer team," he'd joked, pulling me close. We stayed up late that night, picking out names, planning nursery themes, dreaming of Saturday mornings with tiny feet pattering down the hallway.

But then he got the job, and suddenly our conversations about the future became conversations about overtime and missed dinners and lack of quality time. The dreams of a family faded into schedules and separate lives. When did we stop dreaming together? When did "someday" become "never"?

My fingers trace patterns on the couch arm, remembering how we used to sit here every evening.

He'd tell me about his day at work, I'd show him my latest paintings. Sometimes we'd just sit in comfortable silence, his hand playing with my hair. Now the silence in this house feels like a physical weight.

The worst part is, I can't even pinpoint the exact moment things changed. It wasn't one big fight or betrayal. We just… drifted. Like boats that slowly slip their moorings, barely noticeable until you look up one day and realize you're lost at sea.

Maybe if he hadn't taken the job, we'd still be together. Still be that young couple who spent weekends picking out paint colors and arguing over where to hang pictures. Still be the people who couldn't fall asleep without saying "I love you" three times, like a magic spell to ward off bad dreams.

The crackers taste stale, but I force myself to eat a few. We used to talk about having twins ourselves—they run in his family. He'd even picked out names: Emma and Olivia for girls, Lucas and Noah for boys. Now those names float in my mind like ghosts of a future we'll never have.

Suddenly, the crackers turn to ash in my mouth. I barely make it to the bathroom, retching into the toilet. Everything spins as I kneel on the cold tile, tears mixing with sweat on my face. This feels different than stress or grief. This feels like…

I reach for the hand towel, but it's not on the rack. I grab some toilet paper and clean my mouth. The bathroom closet feels miles away, but I manage to stumble to it, pulling open the door.

That's when I see them. The box of my brand new pads, pushed to the back corner, untouched for… how long?

My hands shake as I count backward. One month since the divorce. Two weeks before that when… but no, even before then…

Oh god.

The room tilts sideways as realization hits. I grip the counter, staring at my reflection in the mirror. The pale face looking back at me holds the same wide-eyed panic I feel rising in my chest.

I reach into the back of the closet, behind the extra shampoo bottles and old makeup bags, to where I'd hidden a small box months ago. Back when Jeremy and I were still trying for that future we'd planned. Back when we thought we had forever.

The pregnancy test feels heavy in my trembling hands. How many of these have I taken over the years? Always negative. Always followed by Jeremy's gentle "Next time, baby. It'll happen when it's meant to."

Three minutes. That's what the instructions say. Three minutes to find out if my life is about to change all over again.

I pace the small bathroom, counting tiles, counting seconds, counting heartbeats. The test sits on the counter like a time bomb. Through the window,

When the timer on my phone finally chimes, I almost can't look. I almost don't want to know.

But I force myself to turn, force myself to pick up the plastic stick that holds my future in its tiny window.

Two lines.

Clear as day.

Positive.

My eyes find my reflection again, but this time the face looking back at me holds a different kind of panic. Because this isn't just about me anymore.

I'm pregnant.

Chapter Fifteen

Hot water pounds against my shoulders as I press my forehead against the shower wall. Steam fills the bathroom, but it does nothing to quiet the chaos in my mind. How am I supposed to tell him? How do you even start that conversation?

The water runs down my face, mixing with tears I didn't realize I was crying. All those months we tried, all those negative tests, and now... now that we're over, now that he's gone, my body decides it's time?

I turn the water temperature up higher, as if I could burn away the reality of my situation. My hand drifts to my stomach. There's a life growing inside me. Our child. A piece of us that will exist even though we don't anymore.

After the shower, wrapped in a towel, I force down a piece of dry toast. The nausea isn't as bad when I eat something plain, keep my stomach from getting too empty. Mom used to say that about morning sickness too–one of the many pieces of advice she'd shared before cancer took her.

My feet carry me to my art room before I consciously decide to go there. The door creaks as I push it open–how long has it been? Dust motes dance in the beam of light as I pull open the blinds. The room smells of dried paint and possibility.

A blank canvas sits on my desk, patient, waiting. Like it knew I'd come back, eventually. I grab a pencil, letting muscle memory guide my hand. No pressure, just simple lines. A cardinal takes shape under my strokes–like the ones I see at Mom's grave. A butterfly joins it, delicate wings spread in flight.

Mom would know what to do about the baby. She'd hold me while I cried, then make tea and help me figure out a plan. But she's gone. My dad… well he's also gone.

I was five when he left. Old enough to remember his laugh, the way he'd swing me up onto his shoulders, but too young to understand why he never came back. Mom found out he was cheating with his secretary–such a cliché it almost seems made up. He moved to California with her, started a new family. Never called, never wrote.

Sometimes I wonder if he ever thinks about me. If he knows mom died. If he cares. Twenty-five years of silence says probably not. I may try to find him one day.

I prop the finished piece against the wall,

studying it. Two creatures that shouldn't go together–a cardinal and a butterfly–sharing the same space peacefully.

My hands shake slightly as I pull out my phone and open FaceTime. Lilly's face appears after two rings.

"Hey stranger! I was just about to–wait, are you in your art room?"

I nod, trying to smile. "Yeah, I... Lil, I need to tell you something."

Her expression shifts immediately to concern. "What's wrong?"

"I..." My voice catches. Come on, Alexis. Just say it.

"I'm pregnant," I whisper, the words tumbling out just as a shadow falls across my doorway.

The metallic clatter of keys hitting the floor makes me flinch. I look up to find Jeremy frozen in the doorframe, one hand still raised where his keys had been. His face drained of color.

"I'll... call you back," I tell her before ending the call.

His eyes move from my face to my stomach and back again, like he's trying to solve a complex equation.

I wrap my arms around myself, suddenly cold despite the August heat seeping through the windows. The dust from his work boots spreads across the hardwood floor as he shifts his weight–he must have come straight from the job site.

"I..." His voice cracks. He clears his throat and tries again. "I should..." He gestures vaguely at his fallen keys but doesn't move to pick them up.

More silence. The ceiling fan whirs overhead, stirring the air between us. A bead of sweat rolls down his temple, leaving a clean line through the workday grime on his face.

"When..." He stops, shakes his head. Starts again. "I mean..." Another head shake.

He takes half a step into the room, then stops, like he's hit an invisible wall. His eyes catch on my painting–the cardinal and butterfly. Something flickers across his face.

"You're drawing again," he says finally, latching onto this safer topic like a lifeline.

"I've been at it here and there." My voice sounds strange to my own ears. "Needed to... to do something today to distract myself."

His hand goes to his hair–that familiar nervous gesture that used to make my heart flutter. Now it just makes my chest ache.

"I should go."

Part of me wants to stop him, to make him stay and figure this out right now. But what is there to figure out? We're divorced. We're having a baby. Both things are true, and neither of us knows what to do with that reality.

"Yeah," I whisper. "Okay."

He bends slowly to pick up his keys, his movement careful like he's underwater. Standing up, he takes one more look at me, opens his mouth as if to say something else, then turns and walks away.

I listen to his footsteps down the hallway, counting them. Thirteen steps to the front door. The familiar squeak of the third floorboard. The door opening, closing.

The cardinal in my painting seems to watch me with its eyes, as if waiting to see what I'll do next. I wish I knew.

Chapter Sixteen

Morning sickness should really be called all-day sickness. I've already thrown up twice, and it's barely 8 in the morning. The bathroom tile is cool against my legs as I sit back, waiting to see if my stomach has settled.

Each wave of nausea is a reminder that this is real. That I'm really pregnant.

My phone sits on the counter. The number for the women's clinic pulled up but not yet dialed. I've been putting this off for days, but I need to make an appointment. Need to make sure everything's okay. Need to make this official beyond three positive home tests.

The call is surprisingly easy. The receptionist is cheerful, matter-of-fact. "First pregnancy?" she asks.

"Yes." I don't mention the divorce. Don't mention that the father doesn't even live here anymore.

"We can get you in next Thursday at 10 AM. with Dr. Larson."

I add the appointment details in my phone's calendar.

"Okay, thank you." I say and hang up. The toast I manage to eat tastes like cardboard, but it stays down. Small victories. I've started keeping crackers by my bed, learning to eat before I even sit up in the morning. My body is already changing its routines, and I'm just trying to keep up.

Seven days since Jeremy found out. Seven days of silence. I check my phone again–no messages from him, none from Lilly, either. What is going on? The house feels emptier somehow, like the news has created a vacuum that's sucking all the air out.

I spend the morning cleaning, trying to keep my hands busy. The kitchen first, then the living room. When the doorbell rings, my heart leaps into my throat when I open it to see him standing on the porch, hands in his pockets, looking as nervous as I feel. No orange work shirt today–just a plain grey t-shirt and jeans. He looks younger somehow.

"Hey," he says softly. "Can we talk?"

I step aside to let him in, noting how he hesitates at the threshold, like he's not sure if he belongs here anymore. We end up in the kitchen–neutral territory.

"I've been thinking," he starts, leaning against the counter where he used to eat breakfast every morning. "About us. About everything."

"Jeremy—"

"Let me finish, please?" His eyes meet mine, earnest and familiar. "I know we can't just pick up where we left off. I know it's complicated. But maybe… maybe we could try taking things slow?"

I wrap my arms around myself. "I don't know if that's a good idea right now."

"Not getting back together," he clarifies quickly. "Just… talking. Being in each other's lives again. For the baby, but as well…" He trails off, gesturing vaguely between us.

A memory surfaces, unexpected but vivid. Complete change of subject. "Remember, Mr. Thompson's golf clubs?"

His face breaks into a surprised grin. "Senior year. God, we covered his whole car in golf balls."

"You said they'd just roll off!" I can't help laughing at the memory. "They got stuck in his windshield wipers."

"Hey, that was Kyle's idea. I just provided the golf balls."

"From your dad's collection."

"Which he never noticed, by the way." He slides down to sit on the kitchen floor, like we used to do during late-night talks. After a moment's hesitation, I join him.

"Remember Ashley Carson's graduation party?" he asks.

"When Tom fell in the pool with his phone?"

"And the cops showed up because the neighbors complained—"

"—about the karaoke!" we finish together, dissolving into laughter.

The tension eases as we trade memories back and forth. Senior prom, when his boutonniere fell apart, and we had to safety pin it together. The time we got lost driving to the beach and ended up two states over.

"Our wedding," he says softly, and the air shifts. "Dad was so proud to walk you down the aisle."

I swallow hard. "He was the closest thing I had to a father. Is," I correct myself. "The closest thing I have."

"He asks about you, you know. Mom, too."

Nodding, I pick at a loose thread on my shirt. "I haven't heard from Lilly since… since last week. When you overheard."

Jeremy's posture stiffens slightly. "Oh?" His tone is carefully neutral, but something flickers across his face.

"Yeah, it's weird. She usually checks in every day, but…" I study his expression. "What?"

"Nothing." He says it too quickly. "Just… nothing."

Silence settles between us, heavier than before. The kitchen clock ticks away in seconds, reminding us that this moment, like all moments, must end.

Finally, he pushes himself to his feet. "I should go. Early shift tomorrow."

I stand too, brushing off my jeans. "Yeah, okay."

We walk to the door together, our footsteps

echoing in the quiet house. At the threshold, he turns.

"Thanks for talking," he says simply. "It was nice."

"It was," I agree.

No hug. No kiss. Just a gentle "Bye, Lex" and he's gone, leaving me with memories of golf balls and proms and weddings, and questions about why he tensed up at Lilly's name.

Through the window, I watch his truck pull away. I touch my stomach absently, thinking about how this baby will have their own memories someday. Their own stories about high school pranks and first loves. Will they have Jeremy's laugh? My stubbornness?

Chapter Seventeen

Thursday, 10 AM. First prenatal visit. I've been staring at my phone's calendar for a few minutes, my phone heavy in my hand.

He should know about it. Should have the chance to be there. But my finger hovers over his name in my contacts, uncertain.

Before I can talk myself out of it, I hit call.

"Lex?" He answers on the second ring. "Everything okay?"

"Yeah, I…" I trace the edge of the appointment card. "I have my first OB appointment on Thursday. I thought… maybe you'd want to come?"

The silence that follows feels endless.

"What time?" His voice is soft, careful.

"Ten. But you don't have to—"

"I'll be there. I can pick you up at nine?"

"Oh." I hadn't expected that. "Yeah, okay."

Another pause. "Thank you," he says finally. "For asking."

"Yeah. Well… see you Thursday."

I hang up before the silence can get awkward again.

Thursday morning dawns hot and sticky, typical August weather. I'm already queasy, but it's nerves as much as morning sickness. His truck pulls up at exactly nine.

"Morning," he says as I climb in. There's a paper bag on the seat between us. "I brought crackers. Mom always said they helped with morning sickness."

The gesture catches me off guard. "Thanks."

The drive is quiet, but not uncomfortable. At a red light, I catch him glancing at my stomach, still flat under my loose shirt. I wonder if he's trying to picture it growing, like I do every morning in the mirror.

The waiting room is full of pregnant women in various stages, some with partners, some alone. We sit side by side, not quite touching, both pretending to read magazines while stealing glances at the other couples.

"Alexis Kline?"

We both stand automatically. The nurse gives us a warm smile, not batting an eye at our obvious awkwardness.

"First baby?" she asks as she leads us back.

"Yes," we say in unison, and follow her.

The exam room is small, forcing us to be closer than we have been in weeks. Jeremy stands by the window while I change into the paper gown, both of us hyperaware of each other's presence.

"The doctor will be in shortly," the nurse says, closing the door behind her.

Jeremy clears his throat. "So, um, how have you been feeling?"

"Sick. Tired. The usual, I guess."

He nods, shuffling his feet. "Mom had terrible morning sickness with all of us. She swears by ginger ale and saltines."

"You told them?"

"No, just... remembering the stories."

Before I can respond, there's a knock and Dr. Larson enters, a cheerful woman with grey-streaked hair.

"Hello! I'm Dr. Larson. " She shakes both our hands. "Let's look at this little one, shall we?"

The gel is cold on my stomach. Jeremy moves closer to me as she positions the ultrasound wand.

"There we are," she says, pointing to the screen. "See that brief flicker? That's the heartbeat."

When I see the small little blob on the screen, I

couldn't help but smile. Jeremy's hand finds mine without either of us meaning to.

"Strong heartbeat. Everything looks perfect."

I'm crying, I realize distantly. His hand tightens around mine.

Our baby. A piece of us that exists despite everything.

The drive home is different. Something has shifted, though I'm not sure what. Jeremy holds the ultrasound photos like they're made of glass.

"I can make you copies," I offer as he pulls into my driveway.

"Yeah?" His smile is soft, genuine. "I'd like that."

He walks me to the door.

"Thanks again," he says, "for letting me be there."

"Of course. It's your baby too."

He nods, looking like he wants to say more. Instead, he hands me the crackers from earlier.

"Here, snack on them when you need to." He strolls back to his truck and I watch him disappear around the corner, then go inside and place the ultrasound photo on my fridge. The black and white blob with its flickering heartbeat.

My phone buzzes with a text from Jeremy:

JEREMY

Let me know about the next appointment?

ME

I will.

Chapter Eighteen

THE ULTRASOUND PHOTO HAS BEEN ON MY FRIDGE FOR A week now, held up by the magnet from our honeymoon in Florida. Every morning, I stare at it while my ginger tea steeps. Sometimes I catch myself touching it, tracing the tiny outline of our baby with my finger.

Jeremy's been texting more since the appointment. Little things, like asking if I'm eating enough or sending links to pregnancy websites. This morning it was a photo of a bag of oranges:

Jeremy

Read this helps with morning sickness. Want me to drop some by?

It's strange how normal it feels, this new version of us. Not quite together, not quite apart. Just… connected. Always connected now.

I try Lilly's number again while I wait for my tea

to cool. Straight to voicemail, like every other time this week.

"Hey, Lil. I miss you. I went to my first doctor's appointment yesterday and… well, I wish you'd been there. Or at least answering your phone. Please call me back?"

My voice cracks at the end. Two weeks of silence. Not like her at all. I've driven by her house twice, but her car's never there. Even stopped by the boutique where she works, only to be told she's taken some personal time.

The doorbell interrupts my thoughts. Jeremy stands on the porch with a paper bag of oranges, looking uncertain.

"I was in the neighborhood," he says, which we both know is a lie—his work site is across town. "Thought you might want these."

"Thanks." I step aside to let him in. "Want some tea?"

He hesitates for just a moment before nodding. We move around the kitchen in a familiar dance, him getting mugs while I pour the tea. Like muscle memory—five years of marriage doesn't just disappear.

"Crazy to know we have a little bean coming," he asks, noticing the ultrasound on the fridge.

"Yeah. I can make you a copy today."

"I'd like that." He sips his tea. "Have you told anyone yet?"

I shake my head. "Just Lilly. Well, sort of. When

you overheard." I peel an orange, focusing on keeping the rind in one piece. "Have you?"

"No." He watches me separate the orange segments. "Feels weird, keeping it from everyone. But also…"

"Like it's just ours right now?"

He nods. We sit at the kitchen table in silence, not really much to say since the divorce.

All there really is to talk about right now is our baby.

The morning passes quietly until his phone buzzes. "Work," he says, standing. "I should go."

I walk him to the door. At the threshold, he turns.

"Let me know when the next appointment is?"

I nod. "Of course."

After he leaves, I try Lilly one more time. Still voicemail. This time I don't leave a message.

The rest of the day passes slowly. I research nursery colors, make lists of things we'll need. Around sunset, my phone buzzes with another text from Jeremy:

JEREMY

How are you feeling? Did the oranges help?

I stare at the message for a long time. There's something so intimate about his concern, despite everything.

ME

A little. Thanks.

JEREMY

Good. Get some rest.

I curl up on the couch with my phone, scrolling through old photos of Lilly and me. Birthday parties, beach trips, my wedding day. Her smile was bright and constant through every picture.

"Where are you?" I whisper to her image. "What's going on?"

Outside, a car door slams, and for a moment my heart leaps. But it's just the neighbors. My house stays quiet, my phone stays silent, and I'm left with nothing but questions and the faint taste of oranges on my tongue.

Later, in bed, I find myself on Facebook, looking at Lilly's profile. Her last post was two weeks ago—a photo of coffee and a book, nothing unusual. No clues about why she's disappeared.

I rest my hand on my stomach, taking comfort in this new constant in my life.

"Your aunt Lilly would be so excited about you," I tell my belly. "If she'd just answer her damn phone."

IT'S STRANGE HOW TIME WORKS—HOW MOMENTS THAT once seemed impossible slowly become your new normal. Like Jeremy's work boots by the front door every morning, or his toothbrush back in the bathroom holder. Not in its old spot, but in the spare holder I bought at Target last week. Little boundaries, invisible lines, we both respect.

Three weeks can change everything.

He started sleeping on the couch after that particularly bad Tuesday when I couldn't stop throwing up. "Just to help," he'd said, looking uncertain with his pillow tucked under his arm. Now it's become our routine. Every morning, he folds the blanket neatly over the back of the couch before heading to work. Every evening, he unfolds it again, settling in for another night of being my on-call morning sickness support.

The garbage cans are always lined with fresh bags. The ginger ale in the fridge never runs low. When I stumble to the bathroom at 3 AM, I often find him already awake, ready with a cold washcloth and quiet support. We don't talk about how he seems to sense when I'm about to be sick before I do. About how easily we've fallen back into orbiting each other's lives.

Sometimes I catch him staring at the ultrasound photo on the fridge, his expression soft in a way that makes my heart ache. Sometimes he catches me watching him stare, and we both look away quickly, pretending we don't notice how domestic this all feels.

We haven't told his parents yet. Haven't told anyone, really. It's like we're living in this bubble where only three people exist–him, me, and this tiny raspberry-sized person we made. The pregnancy books pile up on the coffee table–his medical ones mixing with my more holistic guides. We're learning this dance together, this careful choreography of co-parenting while divorced. Of building something new from the ashes of what we lost.

Tonight, like every night lately, I listen to him settling on the couch below my bedroom. The familiar creek of springs, the soft rustle of blankets. Close enough to help if I need him, far enough to remember why he's not beside me instead.

My hand rests on my still-flat stomach, and I wonder if the baby can sense how complicated this all is. If they know that their parents are trying so hard to get this right, even if we got so much wrong before.

We're not together. We're not apart. We're just... here. In this space between what was and what will be. Taking it one day at a time, one craving at a time, one shared smile over a raspberry-sized revelation at a time.

And somehow, it works. For now, it works.

Chapter Nineteen

The doorbell catches me in the middle of my afternoon cracker snacking and-nap routine. I walk towards the door and open it.

Lilly stands on my porch, looking smaller somehow. Her usually perfect hair is pulled back in a messy bun, and she's wearing oversized sweats–something I've rarely seen her do in public.

"Hi," she says when I open the door, her voice rough like she's been crying. "I'm sorry I've been… gone."

I want to be angry. Want to demand where she's been, why she disappeared when I needed her most. But she looks so broken standing there that I just step aside and let her in.

We end up in the kitchen, where I've spent most of my time lately thanks to constant nausea. The silence stretches between us as I make us some tea.

"Zeke and I broke up," she finally says, staring into her mug. "About three weeks ago."

"Oh, Lil." The anger I felt melts away. "Why didn't you tell me?"

She shrugs, and I notice how her shoulders curve inward. "I couldn't... I couldn't talk to anyone. Could barely get out of bed some days." Her voice cracks. "Eight years together, and suddenly it's just... over."

I reach across the table and take her hand. It's cold despite the warm mug she's holding.

"I was embarrassed," she continues. "Here you were going through your divorce, being so strong about it, and I couldn't even handle a breakup. Then when I heard about the baby..." she trails off, blinking back tears.

Her hand drifts to her stomach in a gesture so familiar I almost miss it. Almost.

"Lilly?" My voice comes out barely above a whisper.

She meets my eyes, fresh tears spilling over. "I'm pregnant too." The words tumble out in a rush. "Found out right before... before everything fell apart with Zeke."

"Oh, my god." I squeeze her hand tighter. "Does he know?"

She shakes her head, wiping her eyes. "I tried to tell him, but... it was already over. He'd already decided we wanted different things."

Something flickers across her face when she says this, gone so quickly I might have imagined it.

"That's why I couldn't face anyone," she says. "Couldn't pretend to be okay when everything was falling apart. And then hearing about your pregnancy..." She stops, swallowing hard.

"How far along are you?"

"A couple of months." Her hand stays on her stomach, protective. When she notices me watching, she quickly drops it to her lap.

"We can be pregnant together," I say, trying to lighten the mood. "Our babies will be so close in age."

Her smile doesn't quite reach her eyes. "Yeah."

Through the window, I can see Jeremy's empty parking spot–he won't be back from work for hours. Lilly follows my gaze, then quickly looks away.

"Tell me about your baby," she says, changing the subject. "How are you feeling?"

So I do. I tell her about the morning sickness that lasts all day, about the ultrasound appointment, about my strange cravings for pickles dipped in chocolate (which makes her nose wrinkle just like it should).

"I'm so happy for you," she says softly, though something in her expression seems strained. "You're going to be an amazing mom."

We spend the afternoon catching up. She tells me about the breakup–how she and Zeke had been growing apart, how they wanted different things, how it was mutual but still devastating. I notice she doesn't give many details, but I don't push. Everyone processes grief differently.

"I should go," she says eventually, glancing at the clock. "I start back at work tomorrow."

At the door, she hesitates. "Is… is Jeremy around much? With the baby and everything?"

"Sometimes," I say carefully, noting how she tenses slightly at his name. "He's been helping."

She nods, not quite meeting my eyes. "That's good. He should be involved."

I watch her drive away, feeling unsettled but not sure why. Maybe it's hormones, or maybe it's the way her story seemed rehearsed somehow. Or maybe I'm just being paranoid.

My phone buzzes with a text from Jeremy.

JEREMY

Coming by after work with soup.

ME

Soup sounds perfect.

I'm probably going to throw it up after eating it.

Later, after Jeremy brings the soup and settles into his spot on the couch with his laptop, I tell him about Lilly's visit. About her breakup with Zeke. I hesitate, then add, "She's pregnant, too."

His laptop slips slightly in his hands, but he catches it. "Oh?"

"Seven weeks along," I say, watching his face. But

all I see is the blue glow of his screen reflecting off his features.

"That's… that must be hard for her," he says finally. "With the breakup and everything."

"It's sad. I know me and you aren't together anymore, despite everything I know you wouldn't ever leave me to raise a baby alone."

"Of course."

THAT NIGHT, I LIE AWAKE LISTENING TO THE FAMILIAR sounds of Jeremy shifting on the couch downstairs. My hand rests on my stomach, where our raspberry-sized baby is growing bigger every day.

Everything feels almost perfect. Almost right.

So why does something still feel wrong?

Chapter Twenty

"You're showing a little," he says.

I look down at my stomach, the slight curve visible under my tank top. Almost through the first trimester.

"I noticed it yesterday," I say, running my hand over the bump.

His eyes follow the movement of my hand, something soft and sad in his expression.

"We should probably tell my parents soon," he says carefully.

The thought makes my stomach clench. And not from morning sickness. His mother will have questions. Lots of them. About the divorce, about the timing, about why we're living like this–Jeremy on the couch, me upstairs, trying to co-parent before there's even a baby to parent.

"Maybe after the 20-week scan," I suggest. "When we know everything's okay."

He nods.

"Lilly wants to go baby shopping this weekend," I say, watching his face. "Look at cribs and stuff."

He scrunches his face, but it twists into a small smile. "That's good," he says, too casually. "You two catching up."

"It's weird though. She barely mentions the baby."

Jeremy stands abruptly, carrying his mug to the sink. "I should get to work. Power lines won't fix themselves."

I watch him gather his things, noting the tension in his shoulders that wasn't there moments ago. "Thanks for breakfast," I call as he heads for the door.

"Always," he says, and for a second he looks like he wants to say something else. But then he's gone, the screen door slapping shut behind him.

Later that afternoon, Lilly comes by with some carb filled snacks. "Here's to cravings!"

I laugh and sit down on the couch, her following behind.

"How are you feeling?" I ask, looking her up and down. She doesn't look pregnant yet.

"Fine." She busies herself arranging the vitamins. "Barely any morning sickness."

"Lucky." I lean against the counter. "Have you told your parents yet?"

"No." The word comes out sharp. "Not yet."

"They might be more supportive than you think. About Zeke, about the baby—"

"Can we not?" She cuts me off. "Talk about it, I mean. It's still… raw."

But something in her voice doesn't sound raw. It sounds rehearsed.

"Sure," I say slowly. "Whatever you need."

She relaxes slightly. "Tell me about you and Jeremy instead. How's that going?"

"It's…" I pause, trying to find the right words. "Complicated. But good, maybe? He's been really supportive."

"Has he?" Again, that strange note in her voice.

Before I can question it, she's pulling out her phone. "Look at these nursery ideas I found. I thought maybe we could paint this weekend? Take your mind off things?"

We spend the next hour looking at paint swatches and crib designs.

"I could definitely turn his old office into a nursery,"

"Yes!" she says.

THAT NIGHT, I HEAR JEREMY COME IN LATE FROM WORK. His footsteps pause at the bottom of the stairs. Hours have passed since Lilly left, and the only sounds I've heard are the dull hum of the TV and the occasional distant car.

"Lex?" he calls softly. "You awake?"

"Yeah."

He comes up, stopping in my doorway. In the dim light, he looks younger somehow. More like the boy who used to climb through my window in high school.

"You need anything?" He asks.

I shake my head, "No, I'm okay."

Another pause, heavy with things unsaid.

"Night."

"Night."

I listen to him go back downstairs. My hand drifts to my slight bump, to this tiny life that's somehow brought us closer even as everything else fell apart.

Before I drift off, my phone buzzes with a text from Lilly:

LILLY

Can't wait for this weekend. It'll be good to keep you busy.

I SPEND THE MORNING IN THE SOON TO BE NURSERY— Jeremy's old office–looking at the walls and trying to imagine colors. Sage green maybe, or that soft yellow Lilly suggested. Something neutral, something calm.

A box in the corner still holds some of Jeremy's things–old work manuals, some photos from his training days. I should pack them up for him, but I sit on the floor, sifting through memories.

There's a photo I don't remember–Jeremy at some work function, paper plate of food in hand. The front door opens downstairs, startling me. Heavy footsteps–Jeremy's home early.

"Lex?"

"Up here!"

He appears in the doorway, still in his work clothes, holding a paper bag that smells like our favorite Chinese place.

"Thought we could do lunch instead of dinner. Alex showed up, after all, so I took an early break."

He spots the photo in my hand, and something shifts in his expression.

"Found this in your old work stuff," I say, holding it up. "When was this?"

"Company picnic, I think." He takes the photo, glances at it, then sets it aside too quickly. "You want to eat up here? Start planning this room?"

I let him change the subject, let him spread out the takeout containers on the floor like we're having a picnic. My phone buzzes with a text from Lilly:

LILLY

Still on for painting this weekend?
Picked up some samples I think
you'll love.

ME

Sure!

Chapter Twenty-One

The sizzle of egg wash hitting the counter makes me jump. I wipe it up quickly with a paper towel, trying to focus on the task at hand. My stomach growls at the smell of seasoned breadcrumbs–apparently the baby likes the idea of my dinner choice. The sound of Jeremy's key in the lock startles me. He's early.

The screen door creaks open. God, we never fixed that hinge. Such an annoying sound.

"Something smells amazing," Jeremy calls out. His work boots thud against the floor as he kicks them off.

"Just attempting your mom's chicken parm." I dip another piece of chicken in flour, trying to sound casual. "No promises it'll taste the same."

"Need help?" His voice is closer now. I can smell his familiar mix of laundry detergent and that faint metallic scent that always clings to him after work.

I glance over my shoulder. He's still in his orange work shirt, a smudge of dirt on his cheek making him look younger somehow.

"I've got it under control." I wave a flour-covered hand. "How was work?"

He leans against the counter next to me, close enough that I can feel the heat radiating from his body. "You'll never believe what Caleb did today."

Caleb. He's been working alongside Jeremy all year.

"Oh god, what now?"

"Tried to impress the new accounting girl by showing off on the power lines." Jeremy chuckles, the sound warming the kitchen. "Nearly shocked himself stupid."

"Is he okay?" I toss a piece of chicken into the breadcrumbs.

"Yeah, just his pride that's hurt." He reaches past me for a beer from the fridge, his arm brushing mine. "Though honestly, might've knocked some sense into him if he had gotten zapped."

I laugh despite myself. "Jeremy! That's terrible."

"You're laughing though." He grins, and for a moment it feels like before—just us, in our kitchen, sharing stories about our day.

"Actually," I say, focusing on coating another piece of chicken, "I've been thinking about getting back into art. Maybe try some freelance work?"

"Yeah?" The genuine interest in his voice makes me look up. "Digital stuff like you used to do?"

"Mm-hmm. I love art and–"A cloud of flour poofs up from the chicken, making me cough.

"Careful there, Picasso." Jeremy moves closer, peering over my shoulder. "Though I guess artists are supposed to be messy, right?"

"Oh really?" Without thinking, I flick the flour back at him. It lands on his shirt, white dust against orange.

His eyes crinkle at the corners–that look that always meant trouble in high school.

"Did you just…" His fingers find my sides.

"Jeremy, don't you dare—" But I'm already laughing as he tickles me. "Stop! The chicken's going to—"

"Going to what?" He tickles harder, and I squeal, trying to squirm away.

"You're impossible!" I gasp between laughs, my hands leaving flour prints on his arms.

Jeremy's arms go around me instantly, steadying me. Suddenly, we are face to face, both breathing hard. A piece of hair falls in my face, and he reaches up to brush it away, leaving a streak of flour on my cheek.

"Lex…" His voice is soft, uncertain.

I want him back so badly, though right now it's not the greatest idea. But then his lips are on mine, and thinking becomes impossible.

He tastes like coffee and mint gum. His hand cups my cheek, thumb stroking flour from my skin. My fingers curl into his shirt, and I feel his heart pounding against my palm.

The kiss deepens, and for a moment I'm lost in the familiar way he holds me, the scratch of his stubble against my chin.

I pull back, breath catching. "We should…"

"Yeah." He steps away, running a hand through his hair. "I'm sorry, I shouldn't have—"

"No, it's…" I wrap my arms around myself. "It's not that. Just…"

"Too fast?"

I nod, grateful he understands. "Maybe we could just… take it slow?"

The corner of his mouth lifts in a small smile. "One day at a time?"

"One day at a time." I look around at the flour-covered kitchen and can't help but laugh. "Though maybe we should clean this mess up first."

"Probably safer than whatever we were just doing." He grabs paper towels from the counter.

Later, after we've cleaned up and salvaged dinner, we sit at the kitchen table like we used to.

When he heads to the couch for the night, his lips brush my cheek–gentle, asking nothing. "Night, Lex."

"Night," I whisper back, watching him go.

In bed, I press my hand on my belly. "Your daddy's going to drive me crazy," I murmur.

CHAPTER TWENTY-TWO

I SIT CROSS-LEGGED ON THE FLOOR OF JEREMY'S OLD office, sketchbook open in my lap. The morning light streams through the window, catching dust motes that dance through the air.

I stare at the blank page. I've spent the past twenty minutes trying to come up with a business plan. The words "Freelance Services" stare back at me, underlined twice, followed by nothing.

"Come on, Alexis," I mutter, tapping the pencil against the paper. "It's not that hard."

But it is hard. Every time I try to write down what I could offer–digital design, custom illustrations, brand work–my throat gets tight. What if I'm not good enough? What if I've been out of the game too long?

The doorbell startles me from my spiral. I get up to open the door to see Lilly standing on the porch with two takeout bags from our favorite deli and a stack of magazines.

"Thought we could use brain food for nursery planning." She breezes past me into the house, her perfume lingering in her wake–something new, sharper than her usual scent.

"You're a lifesaver." I follow her upstairs to the office. "I've been stuck up here all morning trying to work on business ideas."

"Oh, show me!" She settles onto the floor, pulling out containers of pasta salad.

I hand her my pathetically empty list, watching as she scans it. "Not much to show."

"Are you kidding? You're crazy talented, Lex." She hands the notebook back. "Remember that logo you designed for my sister's bakery? People still ask about it."

"That was years ago." I accept the fork she offers, stabbing at a piece of tortellini.

"So? It's like riding a bike." She spreads magazines across the floor between us. "You just need to get back on."

"Oh my god," she laughs, holding up a picture of an over-the-top safari-themed room. "Can you imagine? Your poor baby would have nightmares."

"Jeremy would have a fit. He hates anything too busy."

"Speaking of Jeremy…" Lilly sets down her fork, something shifting in her expression. "Have you two talked about what kind of father he wants to be?"

The question catches me off guard. "What do you mean?"

She shrugs, but there's something deliberate in the gesture. "Just... you know. He works so much. And with the divorce and everything... is he really ready for this?"

"Of course he is." But even as I say it, I notice how she's watching me, head tilted like she's waiting for something.

"If you say so." She turns back to the magazines, flipping pages too quickly to really see them. "I just worry about you, that's all."

The room feels smaller suddenly, I stand, needing to move. "I should open a window."

"It is warm in here. Must be all these pregnancy hormones, right?"

I fiddle with the window latch, and open it up. When I turn back, she's arranging paint swatches in a fan pattern on the floor, humming under her breath. She looks up and smiles–the same smile I've known since high school.

"What about this color scheme?" She points to a soft green. "Very gender-neutral."

We spend the next hour looking at colors and furniture, making lists and rough budget plans. On the surface, everything is normal. But there's an undercurrent I can't quite name, like music playing, just slightly out of tune.

When she leaves, the house feels both emptier and lighter. I return to my sketchbook, staring at the blank space under "Freelance Services." Maybe it's not just fear of failure holding me back. Maybe it's about figuring out who I am now–not just Jeremy's ex-wife, not just a soon-to-be mother, but me. Alexis. An artist.

I pick up my pencil and start writing. No services this time, but dreams. Things I used to love: typography that flows like water, illustrations that tell stories without words, designs that make people feel something. By the time I'm done, the page is full.

It's not a business plan. Not yet. But maybe it's a start.

My phone lights up with a text from Jeremy about picking up dinner on his way over, and I smile. Despite Lilly's questions, I know what kind of father he'll be. I've seen it in the way he researches baby gear, in how he asks about every doctor's appointment, in the gentle way he talks about our future.

THE DAY SLIPS AWAY AS I LOSE MYSELF IN SKETCHING. Random doodles turn into actual designs–a logo for a coffee shop, a children's book character, a typography that swirls across the page. My hand remembers things my brain had forgotten.

The front door creaks open downstairs. "Lex?" Jeremy calls.

"Up here!" I call back.

He appears in the doorway, still in his orange work shirt, holding up a bag that smells like garlic bread. "Thought you might be hungry."

"Starving, actually." I gather papers, trying to create order from chaos.

"Leave it," he says, settling onto the floor next to me. "Show me what you've been working on instead."

Heat creeps into my cheeks. "It's nothing, really. Just experimenting with some ideas."

"These don't look like nothing." He picks up a sketch of intertwined letters. "This is really good, Lex."

"Yeah?" I watch his face as he studies the design. "I was thinking maybe I could start small. Take on a few projects, build a portfolio…"

He looks up, smiling. "About time."

"What's that supposed to mean?"

"Just that you've always been talented." He unpacks the food—Italian from Mario's, my favorite. "Remember that mural you did for the community center? People still talk about it."

"You're the second person to mention that today." I accept the container he hands me, the smell of marinara making my mouth water. "Lilly brought lunch earlier."

Something crosses his face—concern? "Yeah? How

was that?"

"Good. Weird." I twirl pasta around my fork. "She had a lot of questions about you."

"Like what?"

"About being a dad. If you're ready." I study his reaction. "It was strange."

He's quiet for a moment, staring at his food. "What did you tell her?"

"That, of course, you're ready. You're already being amazing about everything." I pause. "You are, you know. Amazing about everything."

His fork stills. "Even though I messed everything up before?"

"We both messed up," I say softly. "But this is different. This is our baby."

He nods, then reaches for my sketchbook. "Tell me about these other designs. The coffee shop one caught my eye."

I let him change the subject, explaining my ideas for local businesses, for children's books, for anything that comes to mind. He asks questions, makes suggestions, remembers details about my old projects that I'd forgotten.

The sun sets as we talk, casting long shadows across the floor. Empty takeout containers litter the space between us, and my hand cramps from gesturing as I explain concepts.

"I should clean this up," I say finally, looking at the mess around us.

"Here." He gathers containers while I stack

papers. As I reach for a fallen pencil, my shoulder brushes his arm. The contact sends warmth through me, familiar and new all at once.

"Thanks for dinner," I say, trying to sound normal. "And for listening to me ramble about art stuff."

"I enjoy hearing you excited about things again." His voice is soft in the dimness. "Missed that."

Before I can respond, a wave of nausea hits—apparently the baby isn't as fond of garlic as I am. I must make some sort of face because Jeremy immediately stands.

"Water?" he asks, already heading for the door.

"Please."

When he returns with a glass and some crackers, I've moved to sit against the wall, head between my knees.

"Morning sickness is such a lie," I groan. "More like all-day sickness."

He sits beside me, close enough that I can lean against him if I want to. "Want me to stay until it passes?"

I want him to stay, but not just until the nausea passes. I want him to stay, period.

"I'm okay," I say instead.

"Okay, I'm going to head downstairs and get ready for bed." He says and kisses my forehead and leaves the room.

Or just stay here with me.

Why can't I just say the words?

Chapter Twenty-Three

Morning light streams through my office window as I sit at my desk, looking at the computer. Portfolio website mock-ups spread across the surface. After last night's talk with Jeremy about getting back into freelancing, I woke up with renewed energy, determined to take actual steps forward.

I'm tapping my pencil against a sketch of potential logos when my phone buzzes. Lilly.

Lilly

Have you thought more about painting the nursery? I'm free today

Jeremy and I hadn't really discussed when we'd start the transformation, though we'd looked at paint samples. Everything between us feels delicate right now, like we're building something fragile and new from the fragments of what broke.

ME

> Not yet. Still working on some design stuff today.

Her response comes quickly:

LILLY

> You can't avoid it forever. Babies come whether the room is ready or not.

Before I can respond, another message appears:

LILLY

> Besides, wouldn't it be better to do it with a friend than your ex?

Ex. The word sits heavy in my stomach. Is that what Jeremy is now? After last night—the way he listened to my dreams about art, how he remembered every detail of my old projects, that moment when he kissed my forehead before going downstairs. It feels odd to call him that.

The sound of the front door opening pulls me from my thoughts. Jeremy's voice carries up the stairs: "Lex? You up here?"

"In the office!" I call back, quickly turning my phone face-down as his footsteps approach.

He appears in the doorway, still in his work clothes despite it being his day off. "Thought you might want breakfast." He holds up a bag that smells like the bakery downtown. "Those chocolate croissants you've been craving."

"You remembered?" The surprise in my voice makes him smile.

"Hard to forget when you texted me about them at midnight." He sets the bag on my desk, careful not to disturb my sketches. His eyes scan the papers. "Making progress?"

"Some." I pull out the still-warm croissant. "I was thinking of starting with local businesses, maybe—" The words catch as a wave of nausea hits. Not morning sickness this time, but that metallic taste that means I'm about to faint.

He places his hand is on my shoulder instantly. "Lex? You okay?"

"Just dizzy," I manage, but the room is already starting to spin. Through the haze, I see him reach for his phone.

"I'm calling the doctor."

"No, I'm fine, really—" But even as I protest, black spots dance at the edges of my vision.

"You're not fine." His voice is firm but gentle. "You barely ate yesterday, you're working too hard, and now you're pale as a ghost. We're getting you checked out."

We. The word echoes in my head as he helps me stand. When did we become we again?

My phone buzzes on the desk—probably Lilly again—but he's already guiding me toward the door, one arm steady around my waist. The half-eaten croissant sits abandoned next to my sketches, dreams and breakfast both interrupted by this new reality.

"I can walk," I protest weakly, but lean into him anyway.

"Humor me?" His voice is light, but I can hear the worry underneath. "After everything we've been through, let me take care of you. Just for today."

Everything we've been through. The words hang between us as we make our way downstairs. There's still so much unsaid, so much we need to figure out. But right now, with his arm around me and his heart beating steady against my shoulder, none of that seems to matter.

As he helps me into his truck, I catch him glancing at my stomach. This is what we lost before, I realize. Not just each other, but moments like this—caring about each other, taking care of each other, being there without question or hesitation.

The hospital lights are too bright, the waiting room too quiet except for the steady beep of monitors somewhere down the hall. Jeremy hasn't let go of my hand, even as nurses come and go with questions and concerned looks.

"Blood pressure's a bit low," one tells us, making notes on her tablet. "How long have you been having dizzy spells?"

"Just today," I start to say.

The nurse nods, adding more notes. "And how's the morning sickness been?"

"Better some days. Worse others." I squeeze

Jeremy's hand without thinking. "Mostly just tired lately."

"That's normal," she assures us. "But let's run some tests to be safe."

As she sets up the ultrasound machine, I feel Jeremy tense beside me. Our last ultrasound was weeks ago, when everything between us was still raw and new. Now he moves closer, his thumb tracing circles on my palm as the cold gel hits my stomach.

The whoosh-whoosh of our baby's heartbeat fills the room. Strong and steady, just like their father's hand in mine.

"Everything looks perfect," the nurse says, but I barely hear her. I'm too focused on Jeremy's face, on the way his eyes shine as he watches the screen.

The nurse prints out ultrasound photos - our tiny baby, growing stronger each day. "The doctor will be in shortly to discuss your blood pressure. Try to rest until then."

Jeremy tucks the photos into his wallet, next to the one from our first appointment. "Remember when we could barely see anything? Now look - actual baby shape."

"I still say it looks like a blob." But warmth spreads through my chest at his excitement.

"A very cute blob." His thumb traces the edge of my palm. "Our blob."

The doctor knocks and enters, chart in hand. "So, Mrs. Kline."

"Ms," I correct automatically. The title still feels strange.

"My apologies. Ms. Kline, your blood pressure's running low. Not dangerously so, but combined with the dizzy spells, I'd like you to take it easier. More rest, regular meals, plenty of fluids."

"I can make sure of that,"

"Good. No heavy lifting, no painting." she glances at my paint-speckled fingers— "and try to keep stress minimal. I want to see you back in a week to check your levels."

Back home, Jeremy insists on making lunch while I rest on the couch. "Grilled cheese?" His head pops around the corner. "With the fancy cheese your mom used to buy?"

"You remember that?"

"Course I do. You used to beg her to get it every shopping trip."

The sandwich arrives perfectly golden, cheese melting just right. We eat in comfortable silence, the afternoon sun warming the living room.

"About the nursery," he says after a while. "Maybe we could hire someone? Save you from the fumes and stuff."

"We can't afford—"

"I got that bonus from work. The one for the big project last month? Let me do this."

The way he says it - not offering to help, but asking to be part of it - shifts something in my chest.

"Okay," I say. "But I get to pick the colors."

"As long as it's not that awful orange Lilly suggested."

We laugh, and it feels good. Natural. Like maybe we're finding our way back to something real, something honest.

That night, as Jeremy settles onto the couch with his pillow, I pause at the bottom of the stairs.

"Thank you," I say. "For today. For everything."

His smile crinkles the corners of his eyes. "Get some rest, Lex. Doctor's orders."

Chapter Twenty-Four

The hunger pangs wake me from an uneasy sleep, my body still adjusting to this new routine of being alone in our bed. The digital clock on my nightstand blinks 3:02 AM – about an hour before Jeremy's alarm would go off for his early shift at the power company. Even now, months into our separation, my internal clock refuses to forget.

I throw off the suffocating blankets, my skin damp with sweat. The house creaks with familiar sounds as I pad toward the kitchen.

The kitchen feels different at this hour - somehow both smaller and more vast without Jeremy's presence filling the spaces between counters and cabinets. I grab an apple from the fruit bowl, its skin cool and smooth against my palm, and reach for a glass of water. That's when I hear it - a voice so quiet I almost mistake it for the house settling.

"I can't talk right now, she's just in the other room."

Jeremy's voice, but different somehow. Softer. More intimate than I've heard him speak in months. My hand freezes midair, the glass forgotten as I strain to hear more. I press myself against the wall beside the living room archway, my heart thundering so loud I worry it might give me away.

"I want to touch you, too. I will be there this weekend."

The words hit like physical blows, each one stealing more air from my lungs. The apple slips from my trembling fingers, and I barely catch it before it can hit the floor and reveal my presence. The world tilts sideways, reality fragmenting like a broken mirror. Each breath feels like inhaling shards of glass.

"I know, yes. I plan to tell her that I'm going on a fishing trip."

A sob claws its way up my throat, and I press my palm against my mouth.

Confronting him now would be a mistake. I need to be calculated, clear-headed. But my mind is a tornado of fragments: every late night at work, his attitude, every random bathroom break that would take hours, is beginning to make sense.

My legs carry me back to the kitchen on autopilot. I brace myself against the counter, its sharp edge digging into my palms, anchoring me to the moment, and quietly head back into the bedroom.

The sound of the shower running fills the house as noon approaches. His phone sits on the kitchen counter where he left it, screen dark.

I shouldn't.

But my feet carry me toward it anyway. My fingers shake as I pick it up, guilt and fear warring in my chest. A message thread with Lilly is right there at the top.

Lilly. My best friend.

My heart stops as I scroll up through months of messages. Nude Pictures. Late-night conversations. Plans made while I slept alone in our bed and when we were together. The truth unfolds in digital blue bubbles, each one more devastating than the last.

LILLY

I love you. I've always loved you.

JEREMY

I love you, too. We'll tell her soon. I promise.

LILLY

The baby... it's definitely yours.

The phone slips from my numb fingers, clattering onto the counter. The baby. Jeremy's baby. Not Zeke's at all.

The shower stops. I hear the curtain rings scrape against the rod, but I can't move. Can't breathe. Can't do anything but stand there, one hand pressed against my own swollen belly, as footsteps approach.

"Lex?" Jeremy's voice catches when he sees me. He's still dripping, a towel wrapped around his waist, another in his hands mid-dry of his hair. His eyes dart from my face to his phone on the counter.

"How long?" The words come out surprisingly steady.

"Alexis—"

"How. Long."

He lets out a shaky breath. "Almost a year."

A year. While I was planning date nights and trying to fix our marriage, while I was pregnant with his child... he was with my best friend.

"She's pregnant." It's not a question.

His face drops. "Yes."

"And it's yours."

"Yes." The word barely a whisper.

I press my hand harder against my stomach, "All those times she came over to help with the nursery... to check on me...when we would hang out... her giving me advice about what to do with us..."

"We were going to tell you." He takes a step toward me. "After the first trimester, we—"

"Don't." I hold up my hand, stopping him. "Don't you dare try to explain how you were going to tell me that my husband and my best friend—" My voice breaks. "That you were going to have a baby with her while I'm carrying your child too."

"I never meant—"

"To what? To destroy everything? To make me question every memory, every moment?" The tears come hot and unstoppable. "Was anything real? Or were you thinking of her every time you held me, every time you kissed me, every time you talked about our future?"

He moves toward me again, but I back away. "Please, Lex, let me—"

"Don't call me that." My nickname feels poisoned now. "Don't you ever call me that again."

I grab my keys from the hook by the door, my purse from the chair.

"Where are you going?" Panic edges into his voice. "You shouldn't drive like this—"

"Like what, Jeremy? Pregnant? Betrayed?" A bitter laugh escapes me. "Don't worry. I won't do anything to hurt your child. Either of them."

The door slams behind me with a finality that echoes through my bones. In my car, I sit with my hands gripping the steering wheel, watching the front door through tears. He doesn't follow me out.

Of course he doesn't.

My phone buzzes in my purse - Lilly's name lighting up the screen. The sight of it makes me want to drive into her house. I start the car, put it in drive, and leave behind the ruins of everything I thought I knew about love and friendship and forever.

My hands shake on the steering wheel as I drive, muscle memory guiding me through familiar streets. I don't realize where I'm heading until I see the cemetery gates rising before me. Usually, I visit in the early morning or at dusk, when the shadows are softer, when it's easier to pretend I'm just having a conversation with her.

I park, turning the car off and walking to her headstone.

"Hi, Mom," I whisper, lowering myself carefully onto the sun-warmed grass. My hand instinctively goes to my belly.

"Jeremy and Lilly... they're having a baby. Just like us." My voice cracks. "A whole year, Mom. They've been sneaking around for a whole year, and I never saw it. How can I be so blind? I can't even see what's right in front of me."

My phone buzzes again in my purse. I've been ignoring the constant notifications - texts from Jeremy, calls from Lilly. Each one feels like another knife in my back.

"What am I supposed to do now?" I trace the dates on her headstone. "Our babies will be siblings. How am I supposed to handle that? How do I look at my child every day and not think about..." I can't finish the thought.

"I wish you were here," I whisper. "I wish you could tell me what to do. Tell me how to be strong enough for this baby when I feel like I'm falling apart."

I press my hand harder against my stomach, feeling the slight swell that's become more noticeable lately. "It's just you and me now, little one." My voice steadies as I say it. "Well, you and me and Grandma watching over us."

Mom always said changes come in seasons - that sometimes you have to let things die for new growth to take root. I never really understood what she meant until now.

My phone buzzes one more time.

JEREMY

Please come home. We need to talk. Think about the baby.

ME

Which one? Yours with me, or yours with my best friend?

The drive home feels both too long and too short. Every stoplight gives me time to second-guess myself, to wonder if I should just keep driving until I hit the coast, find some small beach town where nobody knows me or my story.

Jeremy's truck is still in the driveway when I pull up. Of course it is. Where else would he go? To Lilly's? The thought sends a fresh wave of nausea through me.

I sit in my car for a long moment, watching the porch light flicker.

The front door opens before I reach it. Jeremy stands in the doorway, dressed now, his hair still damp from the shower that feels like it happened a lifetime ago. His eyes are red-rimmed, but I force myself not to care.

"Lex—" He catches himself. "Alexis. Please, can we talk?"

I move past him into the house, keeping space between us. "About what? About how you've been sleeping with my best friend? About how you're having a baby with her? Or about how you both sat in our kitchen, planning our nursery, knowing what you'd done?"

"I never meant for any of this to happen." His voice cracks. "It just... happened."

"Things like this don't 'just happen,' Jeremy." I turn to face him, arms crossed protectively over my stomach. "You made choices. Both of you. Every secret call, every lie, every time you looked me in the eye and pretended everything was fine – those were choices."

He sinks onto the couch, head in his hands. "I know. God, I know. I tried to end it so many times, but—"

"But what? You loved her too much? She needed you?" Bitter laughter bubbles up in my throat. "Or was it just easier to have us both? Me here playing house, her waiting in the wings?"

"It wasn't like that."

"Then what was it like? Explain it to me, Jeremy. Help me understand how my husband and my best friend could do this to me."

He looks up, tears streaming down his face. "We never planned... when you lost the baby last time, I was so lost. Lilly was there, she understood somehow, and one night we just..."

The mention of our lost baby hits me like a physical blow. "Don't you dare. Don't you dare use that as an excuse." My voice shakes with fury. "I lost that baby too. I was grieving too. And instead of being there for me, you went to her?"

"I'm sorry." The words hang in the air, inadequate and empty. "I'm so sorry."

"Your 'sorry' means nothing to me. I'm going to pack some things. I can't... I can't stay here tonight."

He stands quickly. "No, let me go. Please. This is your home. I'll go."

"This stopped being my home the moment I saw those messages." I head for the stairs, then pause.

"Tell her I hope she's happy with her choices. Tell her I hope it was worth it."

In my bedroom, I start packing. Toiletries, my prenatal vitamins from the bathroom counter, some clothes. My hand hovers over the framed photo of Lilly and me at my wedding. With a swift motion, I turn it face-down.

When I come back downstairs with my bag, Jeremy's still there, looking lost in his own home.

"Where will you go?" he asks, his voice rough.

"A hotel." I set my bag by the door. "And then... I don't know. Maybe California. Or Florida. Somewhere far from here." The words come out steady, surprising me with their certainty. "Somewhere I don't have to watch you and Lilly play happy family."

"You can't just leave." Panic edges into his voice. "What about the baby? What about—"

"What about your other baby?" I cut him off. "The one you're having with my best friend? Did you think about that when you were sneaking around behind my back?"

He steps toward me. "Please, we can figure this out. All of us. The kids should know each other, they're—"

"Siblings?" The word tastes like acid. "And how exactly do you think that would work, Jeremy? Family picnics with your two pregnant women? Holiday dinners where I have to watch Lilly hold your hand across the table? Birthday parties where our kids ask why Mommy and Daddy's friend looks at him like she wants to—" My voice breaks.

"I'll do whatever you want," he pleads. "Whatever you need. Just... don't take my child away."

A bitter laugh escapes me.

"Don't try to find me." I grab my bag, my keys. "Don't send Lilly to check on me. Don't call my friends or family asking where I've gone. You lost that right when you decided to start a second family behind my back."

"Alexis, please—"

"I'll have a lawyer contact you about custody

arrangements. That's all you get from me now." I open the door, and look at him one last time. "I trusted you with everything I had. My love, my friendship, my future. And you took it all and gave it to her instead."

"I never meant to hurt you." His voice is barely a whisper.

"But you did. Both of you did." I turn to face him one last time. "You know what the worst part is? Even now, standing here knowing what you've done, part of me still loves you. And I hate myself for that more than I could ever hate you."

With a loud bang, I slam the door and the smell of freshly cut grass fills the air as I rush to my car. I allow myself one last look at the house where I thought I'd raise my family, where I thought I'd grow old with the man I loved.

I start the engine, put the car in drive, and leave behind the ruins of everything I once believed in. This time, I don't look back.

My phone buzzes again.

JEREMY

Please don't go. I love you.

Fuck you.

MORE FROM THE DADDY SECRET SERIES

BROKEN SECRETS - BOOK TWO.

Chapter One

"Kline! Get your head in the game!" Coach Martinez's voice carries across the sunlit field. "That's the third shot you've missed."

The soccer ball rolls pathetically past the goal, joining its friends in a growing collection of my failed attempts. The early morning sun already beats down on the turf, promising another scorching September day. Perfect. Just perfect.

"Sorry, coach."

"Take five. Get some water."

Dragging myself to the bench, I grab my water bottle and check my phone. The salt air has already started to frizz my hair, a daily battle that Mom says I inherited from someone. Checking my phone, I notice a couple text messages from Maya.

MAYA

Where are you??? Dying without my pre-calc study buddy.

Nvm Sophie's helping. But you better have a good excuse for ditching me.

"Everything okay?" Coach asks, settling beside me on the bench. Her clipboard has college recruitment forms peeking out from beneath the daily practice schedule. A group of surfers catches waves in the distance, their silhouettes black against the brightening horizon. "You're usually begging for extra practice time, not missing easy shots."

"Yeah, just..." The medical forms from yesterday's physical are crumpled in my bag, every blank space a reminder of what I don't know. "Doctor stuff."

Above us, seagulls circle the bleachers, probably hoping someone left behind a sandwich from yesterday's game. The ocean breeze carries the scent of salt and sunscreen which always brings me a sense of ease. Coach's expression shifts to that careful look adults get when they think they're being subtle. "Anything serious?"

"Just some forms I need to fill out. Medical history and stuff."

"Ah." More careful nodding. Everyone at school knows the deal - or at least the version Mom lets people believe. Single mom, dead husband or something. It's easier than explaining that I know absolutely nothing about him except that he lives somewhere in Michigan. Probably prepping for fall and removing leaves from his yard while we're here chasing endless summer.

"Have you talked to your mom about–"

"I should get to class," I cut her off, shoving my water bottle in my bag. "Thanks for the extra practice time."

The morning sun casts long shadows across campus as I make my way to the locker room. Westview High School sprawls across prime oceanfront real estate, all open-air hallways and courtyards designed to catch the constant sea breeze. Mom says the school's location is why our tiny beach bungalow cost so much, but it was worth it to give me "opportunities." Whatever that means.

Maya's waiting at my locker under the covered walkway, arms crossed. Her dark curls are still damp from swim practice, dripping onto her WHS Swimming team hoodie. "You missed pre-calc."

"Had practice."

"At seven AM? On a Monday?" She follows me as I swap out books. "What's really going on?"

"Nothing's going on." The medical forms scratch against my arm through my bag. "Just trying to get better for playoffs."

"Liv." She grabs my arm, forcing me to look at her. "You're my best friend. I know when you're lying."

"I'm not-"

"You are. And you suck at it."

The bell rings, saving me from having to respond. "We're gonna be late for English."

"This isn't over," Maya calls after me as I speed-walk down the open corridor, dodging kids on skateboards and couples making out against the lockers. "You can't avoid everything forever!"

Watch me.

I'm sliding into my seat just as Mrs. Devonne starts taking attendance. The classroom windows are wide open, letting in the persistent sound of waves and distant volleyball games from the beach PE class.

Derek Lance drops into the seat next to me, his goalkeeper jersey damp with sweat. Sand dusts his cleats - probably been practicing kicks on the beach again. "You looked rough out there today."

"Thanks. Really needed that confidence boost."

"Just saying." He pulls out his copy of The Great Gatsby, the margins are filled with his messy handwriting. "Everything okay?"

"Why does everyone keep asking me that?" The words come out sharper than intended.

"Maybe because you're acting weird?" He leans back in his chair, that annoyingly concerned look on his face. "And you missed three easy shots this morning. You never miss."

"I had a doctor's appointment yesterday, okay? Just routine stuff." The lie feels heavy on my tongue. "Can we drop it?"

Mrs. Devonne clears her throat from the front of the room, her flowing yellow sundress moving in the breeze from outside breeze. "If Mr. Lance and Ms. Kline are finished with their private discussion, we can begin analyzing chapter three."

Heat creeps up my neck as twenty-five pairs of eyes turn toward us. Derek mumbles an apology and opens his book, but I catch him glancing at me throughout class. He's known me since the 8th grade - probably sees right through my lies.

The rest of the morning passes in a blur of classes and avoided conversations. Through every window, I see surfers catching waves, tourists spreading towels on the sand, locals walking their dogs along the shoreline. Paradise, if you're into that sort of thing.

By lunch, I'm ready to hide in the library, but Maya intercepts me in the courtyard before I can make my escape. The sun sits high overhead now, turning the metal lunch tables into miniature griddles.

"Nope," she says, linking her arm through mine. "You're sitting with us. Sophie's got drama and I need details."

Our usual lunch table sits under a cluster of palm trees, offering minimal shade from the midday heat. Sophie's already holding court with her latest relationship crisis while the rest of the soccer team pretends to care. I slide onto the sun-warmed bench, pulling out the sandwich Mom made this morning.

"He hasn't texted me back in three hours," Sophie

says, her blonde hair somehow perfect despite the humidity. "What does that mean?"

"That he's in class?" Maya suggests, stealing one of my chips. "Like a normal person?"

"But he usually sends at least a heart emoji between periods!"

I tune out the relationship drama, focusing instead on my sandwich. Mom always writes little notes on the paper - today's says "Love you to the moon and back." It's our thing, has been since elementary school.

"Earth to Liv!" Maya waves her hand in front of my face. "Sophie asked you a question."

"Sorry, what?"

Sophie leans forward, her perfect makeup somehow surviving the beach humidity. "I asked if you're coming to Tyler's beach bonfire Friday. The whole team's going."

"Can't. Family thing." Another lie.

"You always have a family thing," Sophie pouts, adjusting her designer sunglasses. "Your mom's so strict."

If only she knew. Mom's the opposite of strict - probably because she spends so much energy pretending everything's normal. Like this morning, when I tried asking about the medical forms over breakfast on our tiny patio.

"Just fill out what you know, honey. The rest doesn't matter."

Except it does matter. Dr. Jensen had been clear

about that - family medical history is important. Heart conditions, genetic disorders, all the things I should know but don't because Mom guards the past like a state secret.

The bell signals the end of lunch, sending everyone scrambling for shade and air-conditioned classrooms. As I gather my things, Derek catches my eye from across the courtyard, pausing his conversation with his team members He mouths "You okay?" and I give him a thumbs up that feels as fake as the artificial grass on our soccer field.

My phone buzzes in my pocket - probably Maya with more questions I can't answer. But it's Mom.

MOM

Hey sweetie, Don't forget your appointment with Dr. Stevens after school. I will meet you there. Love you!

The medical forms feel like they're burning a hole in my bag. Dr. Jensen had been understanding yesterday when I couldn't fill them out, but she'd been firm about needing them by the end of the week. "Family medical history is crucial," she'd said, marking sections in yellow highlighter. "Especially at your age."

My age. Eighteen. Old enough to drive, join the army, to apply to colleges, old enough to know more about where I come from than "Somewhere in Michigan."

As I head to my next class, mom's voice echoes in my head: *"The past is the past, Liv. Some things are better left there."*

The thing is, I'm starting to think she's wrong about that. After all, even paradise can't hide secrets forever.

www.ingramcontent.com/pod-product-compliance
Lightning Source LLC
Chambersburg PA
CBHW032304310726

48973CB00008B/2521